GRAYSON MANOR HAUNTING

Cheryl Bradshaw

This book is a work of fiction. Names, characters, places, businesses, and incidents either are the products of the author's imagination or are used in a fictitious manner. Any similarity to events or locales or persons, living or dead, is entirely coincidental and should be recognized as such.

First edition March 2013
Copyright © 2013 by Cheryl Bradshaw
Cover Design Copyright 2012 © Flip City Books
Interior book design by Bob Houston eBook Formatting
All Rights Reserved

ISBN: 1482741709
ISBN-13: 978-1482741704

For updates on Cheryl and her books:

Blog
cherylbradshawbooks.blogspot.com

Web
cherylbradshaw.com

Facebook
facebook.com/#!/CherylBradshawBooks

Twitter
twitter.com/#!/cherylbradshaw

No part of this publication may be reproduced, stored or transmitted, in any form, or by any means whatsoever (electronic, mechanical, etc.) without the prior written permission and consent of the author.

ALSO BY CHERYL BRADSHAW

Black Diamond Death, (Sloane Monroe Series #1)

Sinnerman (Sloane Monroe Series #2)

I Have a Secret (Sloane Monroe Series #3)

Stranger in Town (Sloane Monroe Series #4)

Sloane Monroe Series Boxed Set (Books 1-3)

Whispers of Murder (Novella)

Praise for Cheryl Bradshaw's Books:

"Cheryl Bradshaw writes with flair and a page turning speed, never getting bogged down in too much detail, but always giving us a clear picture of settings and people."
--Gerry McCullough, Author of the Angel Murphy Series

"Cheryl Bradshaw draws on both genius and talent for storytelling to hide the writing mechanics so well that in retrospect one wonders if they actually read the story or simply watched it unfold like a movie."
--Borje Melin, Reader

"I am an avid follower of the Sloane Monroe series and any of Cheryl Bradshaw's books. I literally count down the days until a new book comes out."
--Beth Sandlian, Reader

DEDICATION

To good friends who have stuck with me,
navigating the way between calm and turbulent seas.
I dare say, I have the greatest friends of all.

ACKNOWLEDGEMENTS

To my team who always makes it happen including my publicist, cover designer, editor, proofers, and formatter…I would be lost without each and every one of you.

Tom Adair, once again I thank you for your forensic advice and expertise and also to forensic anthropologists, Dr. Marcella H. Sorg and A. Midori Albert, PhD.

And to my readers. I wanted to bring you something fresh and new with this new series. I hope you enjoy reading it as much as I enjoyed writing it.

The theme song of this novel is *Ghosts That We Knew* by Mumford & Sons.

In a letter written to Fanny McCullough after the death of her father, Abraham Lincoln offered these condolences:

"In this sad world of ours, sorrow comes to all; and, to the young, it comes with bitterest agony, because it takes them unawares."

CHAPTER 1

Addison Lockhart watched the cab dart back down the dead-end country road, leaving nothing but a billowy dust cloud in its wake. She squeezed her eyes shut, taking a deep breath before spinning around on the heel of her boot. When her eyes reopened, she wasn't prepared for the image before her.

You're here now. You can do this. No more steps back. No more past. And no more death. Only life. Your life. It's time to move forward.

The house was much older than she thought it would be. It was dingy and needed work—a lot of it. Several of the wood shingles were missing from the exterior. A piece of railing on the left side of the porch had been partially ripped off, its jagged pieces forming splinter-worthy spikes. Even so, there was a sense of grandeur behind the tattered facade—something regal in the architectural beauty of the domed turret and multi-gabled, steep-pitched roof. Even with all of its flaws, none of the windows on the house were broken, not even the magnificent stained-glass one in the center of the top floor.

The property surrounding the Queen Anne-style house was heavily wooded, its thick, mature trees stretching over the back of the mountainside. Addison stood silent and still, taking it all in, hoping she'd made the right decision in coming here. An owl sounded in the distance, making her aware of his presence. She glanced into the trees, knowing he could see her, even though she couldn't see him.

Addison looked over the acreage to the house next door, noticing what appeared to be the pitch of a roof peeking through the trees. There was a good distance between the two houses, which was exactly what she was looking for. Peace and quiet. Serenity. No horns honking, no traffic jams, no sirens…just the faint sound of water coming from what she assumed was the Hudson River.

One week earlier, Addison had been seated in a stuffy lawyer's office, only half listening to the man on the opposite side of the desk as he rattled off what she'd inherited according to her mother's will: money, jewelry, the autographed record collection that she'd never been allowed to touch, and a house.

A house?

And not just any house. A manor.

"I don't understand," Addison had said. "My mother owned a manor in Rhinebeck, New York?"

The lawyer simply nodded, his eyes scanning the document for additional information.

"My mother never mentioned it to me before."

The lawyer gazed over the rim of his glasses, staring at her like she was a child who asked too many questions. "From what I understand, it was the home your mother grew up in…or was born in. Are you sure you've never been there before?"

Addison shook her head.

"Says here your grandmother owned the house outright," he continued. "It looks like it has been passed down over the last two generations from mother to child—first to your mother, now to you. There is one curiosity though." Addison lifted a brow. The lawyer continued. "Your grandfather didn't appear anywhere on the deed when it was transferred to your mother. It seems the manor has always been owned by a female."

Addison slouched back into the sofa. "My mother was an only child, and so was I. There wasn't much of a choice."

"Well, I suppose you could just deed it to your father if you don't want to bother with it," the lawyer suggested. "Or you could sell it."

Addison snapped out of the memory and stared back

at the house again, wondering why it had been abandoned for so long, forced to deteriorate year after year. If no one wanted it, why hadn't it been sold? It seemed a shame for such a thing of beauty to go to waste.

She placed a foot on the front porch step, testing its durability by tapping it with the toe of her boot a few times to make sure it wouldn't cave in when she applied more pressure. When she felt confident it would hold her weight, she stepped forward, continuing the ritual on the next step and the next one after that. She made it onto the porch and walked to the front door, stopping to notice a metal nameplate drilled into place over the mailbox. It was too grimy to read. She looked around, seeing nothing she could use to clean it off. She pulled the sleeve of her sweater over her hands and wiped the nameplate down, reading the words aloud as they came into view: "Grayson Manor."

Addison reached into her pocket, pulled out a key ring, and inserted the largest of the keys into the door. It clicked, unlocking instantly, but when she pushed against the solid mass of wood, it didn't budge. She tried again, this time ramming the side of her body into the door, shoulder first. It hopped forward only an inch, the door standing firm, like a bully blocking passage to the other side. She backed up, gripped the handle, and tried again, this time with more force. The door swung open, almost flinging her to the floor in the process. She didn't mind—she'd gotten what she wanted. She was in.

The interior of the house was run down, yet charming, just like the outside. Addison expected to find rooms full of furniture with sheets thoughtfully placed over the top, preserving their integrity. Instead, pieces were haphazardly strewn about in piles, many of them damaged from years of neglect.

Off to one side was a kitchen, although it didn't look much like one. All of the appliances were missing, and the drawers and cabinets contained nothing but layers of dust and rat droppings—some fresher than others. Addison ran a finger across the front of a cabinet door, staring at the cakelike layer of dirt before wiping it off on her jeans. The dark walnut cabinetry was simple yet refined—elegant enough to suggest that great care had been taken to beautify the place at one time. She was determined to make it that way again.

She left the kitchen and entered a large, open living space with wood floors. The room reminded her of a dance hall, large enough for a banquet or a significant-sized party. A trio of sullied chandeliers hung from the ceiling, the one in the center being far more grandiose than the others. It may not have been what she expected, but with a lot of restoration work, she could create the house she'd always wanted. A house she could call her home. It felt good to finally be alone.

The only problem? She wasn't.

CHAPTER 2

After exploring the main level, Addison ascended the stairs, enlisting the same precautions she'd taken on the porch steps outside. At the top, she came to a door. It seemed like such a strange place to have one, but she assured herself it was probably common in older houses. She turned the knob, relieved when it opened with ease. She took a few steps forward and looked around, tapping the air with a finger. "One…two…three…four bedrooms," she counted aloud. Including the ones on the first floor, there were seven bedrooms in all. From what little family history she'd received, Addison had learned an interesting fact: every generation bore only one child. Why then were so many rooms necessary, and what had they been used for?

A mirror in the hall offered the first glimpse of Addison's disheveled state. Her auburn, shoulder-length hair hung in unruly wisps, some curling into her face, others shooting out in various directions, all courtesy of a long ride on a stuffy, overbooked plane. She removed a hair band from her wrist, twisting her hair around it until it formed a loose bun. It wasn't tight, the way she liked, but it would do. For now. The smeared makeup beneath her bright, hazel eyes would have to do as well. Every one of her freckles dotted her face like bits of scattered glitter, something that usually made her very self-conscious. Right now, however, there wasn't anyone around to impress.

Addison had just begun to look around when the hallway door slammed shut behind her, sending a jolt through her waifish frame and causing her to jump back. *That's strange*, she thought. *All the windows in the house are closed.* And she hadn't seen or felt a draft anywhere. She stared at it, considering whether or not to open it up again, when her attention shifted to another door.

The first bedroom on the left had a different door than all the rest. The slim sidelites to the left and right of the center piece made it look a lot more like a front door than an interior one. Oddest of all were the white, roll down shades that covered the sidelites, maneuverable on either side of the door.

She tugged the middle shade to retract it. Nothing happened. Stiff and brittle, the shade almost broke apart in her hand. She pinched the bottom of the shade with the tips of her fingers, lifting it gently. On the outside of the glass, boards had been placed, blocking her view from the room.

Why?

Her curiosity was piqued.

She twisted the handle, hoping to enter the room and explore it further. The door was locked. She pulled the key ring from her pocket and began testing the various keys at the lock. None of them worked.

Frustrated, Addison abandoned the first door and tried the next closest one. To her surprise, it opened. In fact, all the doors in the hall were unlocked—all except the first. Each room was simply adorned with mattresses stripped of bed sheets sitting atop stunning, ornate, metal bed post frames. Night stands on each side of the bed. Nothing more. There were no dressers of any kind, no items on the walls. At least, not anymore. "Where is everything?"

A door creaked open. "My guess, the attic if they've got one," a male voice echoed down the hall.

Addison took a step back and poked her head into the hallway. A stocky, but muscular man wearing tan steel-toed boots, jeans, and a black fleece hoodie with a large cross on the front stood in front of her, his fingers jammed halfway into his jean pockets, thumbs out. He grinned, revealing dimples that seemed to cut deeper as his smile widened.

"Who are you?" Addison asked. "And why do you think it's okay to just walk into somebody else's house without knocking?"

The man walked toward her, a strand of his straight, blond hair falling over his eyelid in the process. He stuck out his hand. Addison stepped back, staring at it for a moment and then back at him.

"I didn't think anyone else was here yet; there's no car out front," he said.

Addison crossed her arms.

The man withdrew his hand. "Maybe we should start over. I'm Luke Flynn. You called me, remember?"

"*You're* the historical restoration architect? I thought you'd be—"

"Older?"

"Something like that."

"I get that a lot," he said. "I'm older than you think. And besides, my age shouldn't make a difference. I'm qualified to do the work you need—isn't that what matters?"

"How old *are* you?"

"How old are *you*?" he shot back.

Addison had guessed he was closer to twenty-five, and several years her junior. She tried to get a good look at him, but the light filtering through the naked window into the room had started to fade. Addison stepped back into the bedroom, flicking the light switch. Nothing happened. "Why aren't the lights working? I called the utility company. The electricity was supposed to be on today. I wouldn't have come here yet if I knew it—"

Luke repressed a laugh. "How long has it been since anyone lived here?"

Addison shrugged.

"Okay...how long has it been since the power was on in this place?" he asked.

"I don't know. I didn't ask. I found the number to the utility company, called them up, and told them to turn it on—today. Maybe they got the day wrong."

Luke shook his head.

"What's so funny?" Addison asked.

"You don't know how this all works, do you?" he said, swirling a finger around in the air.

"Isn't that what I hired *you* for?"

"Yeah, but I figured you'd know something. It is *your* house."

"I'm seeing it for the first time—same as you. Until a week ago, I didn't know this place existed."

"You just bought it?" he asked.

"It was part of an inheritance." She flipped the switch again, as if she expected something magical to happen. "What about these lights, then?"

"I'm going to take a stab at it and say the electricity has been off for a while. Years even."

"What does that mean?"

"My guess—it'll have to be brought up to code before the service can be restored," he said. "You can't just pay a deposit and get the lights turned back on." Luke ran a hand up and down the door frame. "Not in an old beauty like this."

"When can you have everything up and running?" Addison asked.

"Depends."

"On what?"

"What's most important to you," he said. "Is that what you want to happen first?"

Addison nodded.

"There's a good chance I'll need to hire a contractor to rewire the entire house," he said. "I'll take a look around tomorrow and get a better idea. Do you need me to run the cost by you before I—"

"I have the money as long as you're reasonable," she said, flatly.

"I'll make some calls tonight then. What time should I meet you here tomorrow?"

"It doesn't matter—come whenever you want. I'll be here."

He started to turn, until something she said clicked. "Wait a minute—you're not *staying* in this old place—right?"

She hesitated. "I had planned on it. I had no idea it would be in this condition until after I got here."

"There are plenty of decent hotels in the city. I can recommend a few if that will—"

"I don't want to stay in the city." Her coarse words slashed through the air before she could do anything to stop them.

The boxes she shipped wouldn't arrive for another four days, and she was naïve to think she could manage until then with a mere two suitcases, the duffel bag of food she brought, and no car.

Luke backed up, holding his palms out in front of him. "Okay, okay, geez."

"I didn't mean to—I just—I came here to…get away from it all. I'd rather stay in a house that's falling apart than return to where I came from. Besides, I'm already here."

"That bad, huh? Hiding out?"

"What?"

"I can't think of any other reason you'd want to stay here right now," he said. "Not unless you're running away from someone."

Or something—a past life she'd rather forget.

Addison sighed. "It took me all day to get here, and I'm tired. Can we talk about all of this tomorrow?"

"Look—this place isn't even fit enough for you to sleep on the floor right now." He walked into the bathroom and back out again a minute later. "Water isn't working either. You won't be able to shower, and what are you going to eat? I looked at the kitchen when I got here. There isn't a refrigerator or an oven. I don't feel comfortable leaving you here."

"Why? Because I'm a woman? I can manage. I've been on my own for a long time."

"I'm not trying to tell you what to do. I just wanted to help."

She placed her hands on her hips. "Why? You don't even know me."

He shrugged. "Why does that matter?"

"I have a phone," Addison said, her tone confident. "I'll call a cab if I change my mind. But I do appreciate you offering to—"

"Check it," he said.

"What?"

"Your phone—just do it."

Addison plucked the cell phone out of her pocket. The service bars on the screen flickered between one and none. Great. Her new life was already turning out to be a disaster. She knew the house would need to be restored—the lawyer had mentioned it in their meeting—but she never thought it would be this unlivable.

Luke sighed. "What if I find you a place to stay that's close to the city but not in a busy area. Would you consider it?"

"You don't need to do that."

"It would only be for a few days," he insisted. "I'll get the water on and the power and then you can come back. Sound good?"

Addison hated to admit it, but he was right. She couldn't stay here. "Do you have a specific place in mind?"

"A guest house—you'll have plenty of privacy. Let me make a call first and make sure it's okay."

"I thought you said the reception wasn't very good out here?" Addison asked.

"For you, maybe, not for me." He winked and stepped outside.

Addison turned, looked around, and became more aware of how much work it would take to fix up the place. *What have I gotten myself into?*

CHAPTER 3

Two weeks and three days later, Addison returned to Grayson Manor with a new car and a different phone carrier. The guest house Luke had secured for her belonged to his parents, Jim and Bonnie Flynn. It was detached and set back far enough behind the main house that Addison had all the privacy she needed. Still, it didn't stop Bonnie from stopping by every night with an extra dinner plate and an offer of female conversation. At first, Addison politely declined, saying she could make herself a sandwich, but the word "no" wasn't part of Bonnie's vocabulary. Somehow, she always found a way inside Addison's room and her heart, and by the end of Addison's time there, she was eating dinner in Luke's parents' house every night, often with Luke joining them at the dinner table.

Over the past couple of weeks, Addison had made several trips back and forth to check on the progress of

Grayson Manor. Each new day it seemed there was some kind of a new problem that prolonged her return, but eventually Luke declared the home fit enough for her to move back in. There were months of work to be done, but the shower had water, the lights turned on, and the stove could cook a meal. It was progress.

Luke was working on the floor in one of the upstairs bedrooms when Addison arrived. He'd tried to get her to stay on the main level, since they were renovating the upper level first, but Addison preferred the upstairs, saying the view from the middle bedroom was one of the loveliest she'd ever seen. There was no convincing her otherwise.

"It looks great in here." Addison entered the bedroom, marveling at its transformation.

"You are looking at a close replica of what this room originally looked like," Luke said.

"I can't believe this house has been sitting here for all these years when it could have been lived in and enjoyed."

Luke tilted his hammer toward her. "Maybe you should ask whoever left it to you."

Addison had tried not to think about her mother every day since she had died. She tried not thinking about how much she missed her. She tried shutting out the memories of her mother being in the first row for every single one of her volleyball games when she was in high school or when her mother cried when they said goodbye on her first day of college. She tried because trying to forget seemed easier…though she suspected her thinking was skewed. Either way it was like a slow pain, churning and growing inside her body, waiting until the perfect moment to rupture.

"Did I say something wrong?" he said. "You look upset."

She shook her head. "No, it's okay. When I said I'd inherited the house, it was from my mother."

"Makes sense," he said. "She probably wanted to see it put to good use."

"What I mean to say is…she's dead."

It was the first time Addison had said the words aloud since her mother had passed away.

"I'm sorry." He shifted his gaze away from her, looking unsure about whether to continue.

"It was an accident, her death. I can't—I mean, it's hard for me to—"

"It's okay if you don't feel like talking about it. It's not easy losing someone you love."

Had he lost someone? A woman in his life, perhaps? At thirty-one, it was possible. Both of his parents were alive and well, she knew. Yet, there was a trace of seriousness in his tone, maybe a longing for someone.

Not wanting to talk about her mother's death was one of the reasons Addison had yearned for the solitude of the country in the first place. After the funeral, she quickly grew tired of the incessant phone calls and the unexpected drop-ins by relatives or one of her mother's friends. Her mother was gone. She didn't need another one. She didn't want another one. No one seemed to understand.

Luke's attitude was different. He wasn't nosey and insistent like the others. Over the last two weeks, she'd decided he was kind and patient, the sort of level-headed person who never got upset about anything. Being in his presence was a refreshing change from the life she'd just abandoned.

"Addison?" he whispered.

She gazed up, pushing the thoughts inside her head as far back as they could go. "I'm sorry."

"Don't be. Whatever happened, you don't have to tell me."

She walked over to the bed and sat down. "This might sound strange, but I want to tell you, and I haven't talked about it with anyone. Not even my father."

He smiled, wiped his hands on his jeans, and sat on the edge of the bed. "You can always tell me anything."

She sat down next to him, choosing to stare at her hands than at him. "There's no way of knowing what happened for sure, but from what we have gathered, this is what we think happened. My mother was driving home one night after seeing a movie with friends. It was late, around ten o'clock. The street she was driving on wasn't very well lit. There was a kid on a bike dressed in a navy shirt and dark jeans. The bike he was riding was an old Schwinn. The reflectors had fallen off, and his parents hadn't bothered to buy new ones, I guess. My mom's cell phone rang. We think she reached for it, and at some point, it slid off the seat. She bent down to get it, and when she sat back up, she must have caught a glimpse of the kid. She swerved, missing the boy, but in her attempt to keep him safe, she lost control of the wheel. She overcorrected and her car flipped several times before slamming into a ditch. My uncle said when they found her the car looked like an oversized piece of crumpled newspaper."

Luke rested a hand on her knee. "No wonder you wanted to get away."

"I just want to be in a place that doesn't remind me of her."

"That's understandable."

"The city I lived in was the city I grew up in. Everywhere I looked, all I saw was her—in everything. There were so many memories. I wanted to move to a place where I could make my own memories, but as it turns out, this is the house she lived in as a child."

"Did you spend a lot of time together?"

"Not as much as she wanted me to. She tried so hard to see me, but I was always too busy—with my career, with my life, in my relationships. I put her off, saying something like we could always get together "next week." Then next week would roll around, and I'd reschedule again. I learned my lesson a little too late."

"You're putting a lot of blame on yourself," he said.

"One month ago, I was living a completely different life. I thought I knew where I was going and what I wanted. I didn't know anything. It took her dying for me to see what I should have seen all along. How many people live like that—blindly following the path they think they're meant to follow?"

He shrugged. "A lot, I'd guess."

"What made you want to work on houses for a living? Out of all the occupations you could have chosen—why this one?"

"It's my passion," he said.

"Old houses?"

He shook his head. "Not exactly. I see things differently than most people."

"Like what?"

"Tell me something," he said. "What's the first thing you thought of when you saw this house?"

"I didn't expect it to look so...old."

"And?"

"Run-down."

"You saw the flaws," he said. "It's okay. That's what most people see. Your eye naturally goes to the things that need to be fixed."

"And yours don't?"

"I see a piece of fine art," he said. "I see a house covered in many fine layers. My job is to peel them all back, layer by layer, brick by brick, until I uncover the beauty hidden beneath. There's nothing more satisfying to me."

The way his eyes sparked when he talked about doing what he loved gave Addison hope that one day she'd feel the same way about this place too.

"What about you," he said. "What's your passion?"

Addison shrugged. "I don't know. I haven't thought about it in so long, I'm not even sure I have one."

"Everyone does." He gently poked her shoulder. "You just have to be open to it when it finds you." Luke tossed some tools into a box and closed it. "If you don't need me for anything else, I'll head home. See you tomorrow at eight, unless that's too early for you."

"It's fine."

"Most of the window latches were broken when I checked them, so I wedged some pieces of wood in between the frame. It's a temporary fix, but it'll keep them from being opened from the outside. I also installed the new handle you picked out on your front door, so don't forget to lock it."

Addison smiled. "I appreciate it, but I don't think there are too many break-ins out here."

Luke glanced back and smiled. "It's always better to be safe."

CHAPTER 4

Luke had only been gone for a minute or two before there was a knock at the door. Addison opened it. "Forget someth—?"

But it wasn't Luke; it was an older woman with purplish-white curls atop her head. Her hair permanent was the tightest Addison had ever seen. She had a smile that exposed the wrinkles of someone who'd lived a full life. The woman leaned on a wooden cane with one hand and held a pie out with the other. "My name is Helen. Forgive my intrusion, won't you?" She turned, peering at a man in the drivers-side seat of the car parked in front of the house. "I'll just be a moment." Then she looked back at Addison. "I live in the house next door. May I come in?"

"I'm sorry…we're not finished working on the front room, so the furniture hasn't been set out yet. I have nowhere for you to sit."

"That's all right. I'll manage." Helen pushed her way past Addison, depositing the pie into Addison's hands as she walked by. She glanced around the room and grinned. "I'm glad to see someone is taking the time to fix up this place. I spent many nights in this house."

"You *stayed* here?"

"Oh no, dear—not overnight. I'm talking about the parties." She shook her head back and forth. "What fun we used to have. Not a day goes by that I don't miss it."

"The parties?"

Helen wasn't listening. Her eyes surveyed the room while she rambled on about dancing in the parlor room with a man named Harold.

"Did you know my grandmother?" Addison asked.

The realization of who Addison was stunned Helen into complete silence. She turned, staring at Addison like she was seeing her again for the first time. "I knew Marjorie Grayson very well. Are you—Nancy's daughter?"

"You knew my mother too?"

"When she was a little girl, yes. I used to watch her for your grandmother from time to time. She was quite an active little thing, your mother."

"Did she like living here?"

"Of course she did." Helen frowned. "How is it you don't know any of this?"

"My mother never talked about her life here."

"Then how…or why….?" Helen's voice trailed off in her confusion.

"She passed away recently," Addison stated.

"Your mother?"

Addison nodded.

Helen placed a hand on her hip and made a ticking noise with her mouth that sounded like *tkk…tkk…tkk.* "So young. How did it happen?"

"It was an accident—when she died, I learned about the house."

"How?"

"I inherited it."

"What are your plans?" Helen asked. "Will you sell it?"

"I'm fixing it up."

"Yes—yes—I can see that, but then what?"

"I'll live here," Addison said. "I plan to make Grayson Manor my home."

Helen moved closer to Addison and squinted. "You look a lot like your grandmother. I can see that now."

"Did you know her well?"

"We were neighbors…I suppose I did. Shrewd woman, Marjorie."

"Did you just say my grandmother was a rude woman?" Addison asked.

Helen huffed, offended at the implication. "Certainly not."

Addison was sure she'd heard her right, but she let it pass.

"I considered your grandmother one of my closest friends," Helen said.

"Can you tell me anything about her?"

Helen looked around and frowned. "I can, but I'll need to sit." Addison led the elderly woman into the kitchen and found a cushion to place on a wooden chair for comfort. Helen lowered herself down with the natural grace of a royal. "Now. What would you like to know?"

"Everything."

"Surely she's in your life in some capacity—can't you just ask her yourself?"

Addison shook her head. "I've only seen my grandmother once."

Helen's eyes were wide with disbelief. "Only once? Well, when was that?"

"I was very young. She showed up at our house. My mother looked out the window and saw her standing on the doorstep, ringing the doorbell. My mother turned toward me, pointing down the hall. She told me to go to my room, but I didn't. I snuck around the corner, and when my mother wasn't looking, I peeked."

"And what did you see?"

"My grandmother. I knew it was her because my mother called her 'mom.' I'll never forget it. She was dressed in a long, fur coat that went all the way to the ground. She had red, pointy fingernails, red lipstick, and red heeled shoes with rounded toes. Her hair was pulled back into a bun, and she wore big, round sunglasses. She looked like a model in a magazine."

"What did Marjorie say?" Helen asked.

"She asked my mother if she could see me. She said it was important, and that my mother knew why."

"And your mother—what did she say?"

"She lowered her voice and said something too low for me to hear. Then she slammed the door in my grandmother's face."

"How old were you at the time?" Helen asked.

"I'm not sure. Five, I think."

"So young, and yet you remember?"

"My grandmother is the kind of woman one doesn't easily forget—I suppose especially when I realized who she was."

"And you know nothing else about her?" Helen asked. "It's rather odd that your mother would turn her out in such a way."

"Several years after her visit, I was told that my grandmother had died. When I asked my mother for details, she didn't answer. She just said I didn't need to worry about it. I tried asking my dad, and he just said to talk to my mother."

"Marjorie—dead? I hadn't heard. Of course, I never

knew what happened to her after she left this place."

"That's another thing I don't understand. Why *did* she leave?"

Helen opened her mouth as if to speak, then snapped it shut. "I need to get going. I just wanted to come over and introduce myself. We'll talk again. Good luck with your renovations."

Addison tried to respond, but Helen was already limping back to the car as quickly as a woman with a cane could. She offered a slight wave before the car disappeared around the corner. Addison stood on the porch wondering what had spooked Helen enough to flee her home in such a hurry and why she looked like she had something to hide.

CHAPTER 5

A faint but distinct sound penetrated Addison's dream, the noise becoming increasingly louder until it forced her eyes open. She pushed the covers aside and stood up, a cool sensation sending chills throughout her body when the balls of her feet hit the cold floor. She scanned the room for the cardboard box she'd labeled "DRESSER," combing her fingers through it until she found a pair of mismatched socks. She considered rifling around for a matching pair, but it was late, and she was tired. Addison covered her feet and then crept downstairs, listening and waiting for the sound to return again. But the house had gone quiet.

Addison flipped on the porch light and cracked open the front door, crouching down behind it. "Here, kitty, kitty." She listened and waited. "It's all right, kitty. Come on." Several minutes went by without a sound. Addison eventually gave up, wondering if the sound she heard had somehow been part of a realistic dream. She closed the door, wrapped the blanket around her, and started back up the stairs. She'd only taken a few steps before the faint cries started up again. Only this time, Addison was wide awake, making it easier for her to isolate the sound's location. And she realized a couple of things in that moment. One, the noise she heard wasn't coming from the outside of the house as she'd first thought—it was coming from the inside. And two, the noise wasn't a cat's disconsolate cry—it was a woman's. Or at least, what sounded like a woman.

It's not possible. I'm the only one in the house.

"Hello, is someone here?"

Addison felt ridiculous for saying it. Of course no one was there. She knew that, but the cries continued to erupt until they swirled all around her, increasing in intensity as she climbed the stairs. The door at the top of the stairs was closed again, even though Addison was certain she'd left it open minutes before. She reached for the handle, but there was no need; the door creaked open on its own. A rush of cold, stale air blew past her, the force of it causing Addison to grip the handrail beside her and hold on tight.

The breeze soon subsided, the near-violent cries drowning away as the house settled back down again. A frantic Addison darted in and out of each room, opening closet doors and bathroom cabinets along the way. There wasn't much to see—they were all bare, just like they were the day she moved in. It didn't make sense. She had heard something—she was sure of it.

She walked back into the hall, her eyes falling upon the outside of the only room she hadn't checked. Figuring it was still locked, she decided it wasn't even worth the effort to check. Then something stopped her. Out of the corner of her eye, she caught a glimpse of the handle on the locked door. It glowed, pulsating in and out like a heartbeat. Addison's eyes widened, baffled at the display before her. She looked away, shaking her head and whispering, "This isn't real. I know it isn't. It can't be." She halfway opened one eye as she turned back around, too afraid to face what was before her with both eyes open. The knob that had been illuminated only moments before now appeared dull and lifeless, an ordinary doorknob. She considered touching its steel, grey exterior to be sure, but shied away. Instead she waited. Several minutes passed by without another change.

Addison returned to her room and lost herself beneath the covers, listening and waiting, the only sound coming from a clock ticking on the nightstand. It was only when the sun levitated over the edge of the mountain that she finally drifted to sleep.

***

Addison woke again, this time to a light tapping on her bedroom door.

"Who is it? Luke—is it you already?"

"You said eight was okay. Remember?"

She glanced at the time. It seemed like mere moments had passed since she'd fallen back to sleep, and yet it was almost nine in the morning. "Come in."

"Are you up?" Luke said, stepping into the room. "I don't want to bother you—I just wanted you to know I'm here. When you didn't come down, I thought I'd better check before I made too much noise."

She stretched her arms into the air. "You're fine."

Luke paused, staring at her for a moment. "Do you need me to come back later?"

"No, why?"

"It's just…you look…ahh, like you didn't get much sleep last night."

"I feel exactly how I must look then. I had the strangest dream."

"What was it about?" he asked.

"I was walking all over the house listening to this sound. At first I thought it was a wounded cat, but then…"

She stopped herself, realizing what he might think if she continued.

"What were you going to say?" he asked.

"It was just a dream. It's no big deal." His eyes shifted

from her to the bottom of the bed. "What are you staring at?"

"Nothing."

It wasn't *nothing*. He looked as though he might break into laughter at any moment.

"Do you always do that?" he asked.

"What?"

"Wear mismatched socks?" he pointed.

Addison tugged on the blanket, gasping as she looked down. It hadn't been a dream after all.

"Is something wrong?" he asked.

"The day we met, you mentioned the possibility of an attic—is there one?"

"Not an attic exactly. But I did find something."

"Where?"

"Get dressed, and I'll show you."

CHAPTER 6

Inside the last bedroom on the main floor was a flat, rectangular door in the center of the wall. It was around three feet in height and had been hidden behind a full-sized bed. At first glance it looked like nothing more than an accident that happened during the construction of the home, but upon closer inspection, Addison realized whoever put it there must have done so intentionally. The cut out was flush with the wall and had no knob or opening of any kind.

"Are you saying there's a room behind this?" Addison asked.

Luke grinned.

"How do you get in?" Addison asked.

"Press on it."

"What—why?"

"Just do it."

Addison flattened her hand against the smooth

texture of the wall and pushed forward. "I don't understand. Nothing happened."

"I didn't either, at first. Now watch this." Luke balled his hand into a fist and lightly punched the front of the door—twice. It sprung open. "This house of yours is full of interesting surprises."

She suspected his statement was truer than either of them really understood at this point. "Have you been inside?"

"I poked my head in yesterday for a minute. It was too dark to see anything." He reached into his pocket and pulled out a small flashlight. He clicked it on. "Let there be light."

He stepped inside and then turned, holding his hand out. Addison hesitated, twisting her nose up when she glanced inside.

"Come on. It's nothing a shower can't wash off," he said. "I can almost stand up all the way. You'll be fine."

She took his hand, swishing cobwebs away with the other as she stepped forward. They descended several steps until they reached a cold, concrete floor at the bottom.

"It's freezing down here." Addison clenched both sides of her sweater, wrapping it tightly around her.

"Here," Luke said, holding a second flashlight out. "I brought this one for you."

She pressed a button on the side of it, rotated her

body around, and beamed the light throughout the room. Except for the dirt-infested cobwebs dangling from above, the room appeared undisturbed, like a time capsule waiting to reveal its hidden treasures. The space ran the width of the house and was filled with antique trunks, old furniture, and various other items.

"I wonder why they have things stored in a room like this, instead of in an attic," Addison said.

"More convenient, probably." The far corner of the room was lined with several wooden shelves sitting in front of a long brick wall. Luke walked over, grabbed a bottle from a shelf, and blew the dust off of it. He coughed, then angled his light at the object he was holding. "It's a 1940 Chateau Grand Puy Ducasse. The shelves are filled with them."

Addison moved closer. "I guess we know why the room was built. Helen told me she'd attended several parties here."

Luke raised a brow. "Helen?"

"My neighbor. She knew my mother as a child, and my grandparents."

"When did you meet her?"

"Yesterday, after you left."

"Did she tell you anything about them, or about the house?"

Addison shook her head. "Not really. She was an uptight ball of nerves actually. I don't understand why she came by in the first place, other than to poke her nose in my business."

Near a wall to the right was a wooden garment rod. Hanging on the rod zipped into clear, plastic bags, were several dresses. "I wonder if these belonged to my grandmother," Addison said, unzipping one of the bags and running her hand along the fabric. "They look so expensive. How could anyone just leave them here?"

The dress rack was positioned in front of a series of haphazardly stacked boxes, and upon one of these boxes, Addison noticed a bunch of old blankets. One in particular caught her attention. Addison tugged on it, pulling it free. "Look at this," she said to Luke. "Someone embroidered my mother's name on this, and a date."

He walked over, grazing against one of the boxes as he went by. The "side bump" caused a ripple effect. Within seconds, the poorly stacked boxes tumbled to the ground. "Oops." Addison then noticed several long, black chests hidden behind the boxes. "What are those?"

Luke followed her line of sight and walked over to the chests. "They're old trunks of some kind." He knelt down beside one of them and flicked a piece of metal dangling from the front with his finger. It lifted up and then banged back down, making a hollow, clanking sound. "Check this out—it's locked."

"Can you open it?"

"Maybe, if we can lift it out of here. I need more

light."

"What about the others?"

Luke easily lifted the lids of the remaining trunks. "Unlocked." Each contained nothing more than worn blankets, so he looked through them all and returned to the locked trunk. He wrapped his hands around the handle on the side and pulled up. The chest barely moved. "Something's in this one, and my guess is it's not blankets. I can't even lift it. These trunks are heavy enough on their own. Put something in them and they're nearly impossible to move. It's probably the reason why they were left behind."

Addison grabbed the handle on the other side. On three, they both pulled upward. "It's too heavy. My fingers are slipping."

"I have an idea," Luke said. "There's a clear path from us to the bottom of the stairs. Let's see if we can slide it over. I'll grab a board from upstairs, and if we can lift the trunk onto it, we can pull it out of here."

"Won't it ruin the bottom?"

"It might. I guess you need to decide how badly you want to know what's inside this thing."

Several minutes and a great deal of huffing and puffing later, the trunk arrived in the bedroom, intact, except for its scraped bottom and sides. Luke took the lock in his hand and inspected it. "I should be able to get this off with some bolt cutters."

He left the room, returning a minute later.

"You just carry those around with you?" Addison asked.

Luke grinned. "I never know when they'll come in handy." He placed the end of the cutters near the lock and lifted up on the handles. When he squeezed back down, the lock broke off like it was made of nothing more than soft, pliable dough. "Well, it's your house and your trunk. Do you want to do the honors?"

"I don't know why, but I'm nervous."

"Would you like me to do it?"

Addison nodded.

Luke lifted the center latch and they peered inside.

"Photographs?"

"Loads of them from the looks of it," Luke said.

"But pictures aren't heavy."

Luke smacked the side of the trunk. "It's this old thing that carried all the weight—not what was inside of it. It's more solid than the others."

Addison put her hands in, scattering the photos around. "Wait, I feel something else." She dug her hand in deeper, yanking the object upward until it was freed. "It looks like a wedding album."

The white book had a padded, pebbly feel to it, like textured vinyl. On the front cover were the words, "Memories of Our Wedding," in shiny, foil letters. Addison opened it. On the first page was a large photograph.

"Do you know who they are?" Luke asked.

"This woman is my grandmother," Addison said, pointing at the photo. "So the man standing next to her must be my grandfather."

"You've never seen him before?"

"I never knew him, or her, really." She stared at the picture, mentally disagreeing with her neighbor's assertion that she looked like her grandmother. Although striking, Addison saw much more of her own features in her grandfather. They shared the same bone structure, their eyes wide and narrow like a cat, his deep-set dimples mirroring her own.

"I don't mean to pry, but why didn't you know them? Did they die when you were very young?"

Addison told Luke about the one and only time she'd seen her grandmother and about finding out she had passed away years later.

"And your grandfather? What about him?" Luke asked.

"My mother said he left when she was a girl. Apparently she woke up one morning and he was gone. She never saw him again."

"Makes you wonder what happened—why your grandmother left this place, why your grandfather left home."

Addison picked a photo out of the box. "Maybe these

pictures will give me some answers, or at least some indication as to who they were."

Luke patted her knee, then stood up. "Well, there's a lot of work to be done, so I'll leave you to it."

For the next hour Addison sifted through the photos, creating piles on the floor next to her according to the dates penned on the back of the photographs. Some of the photos dated back to the 1920s and '30s, leading Addison to assume the couple in those photographs was her great-grandparents. But the bulk of the photos were of her grandparents, and her mother as a baby. The pictures depicted a vibrant, happy couple—not a relationship that ended as abruptly as it seemed. They appeared content, often seated arm in arm, their faces relaxed and calm. *What happened to you two?*

Another hour passed before Addison reached what she thought was the last layer of photos. She scooped them up, bending over the top of the chest to make certain there weren't any she had missed. But instead of a rusty bottom—what she expected to see—she saw a long, white box. She set the photos to the side, gently removing the box from its resting place. She lifted the lid. Folded in half was a vintage party dress. It was tan and had a sheer white overlay. Hibiscus flowers adorned the front, but even more than that, scattered all over the dress were splotches of reddish-brown stains. She leaned in, trying to make sense of the marks on the dress. What were they? How did they get there? And why had someone stored the dress with such obvious stains? She brushed the tips of her fingers over one of the stains, and the room went black.

CHAPTER 7

Out of the darkness, a round, luminous beacon of light appeared. It was small, no larger than a car's headlight. As the moments passed, it grew, shifting several times until most of the room was enveloped in its glow. An image sparked to life in front of her. A young lady who appeared to be in her late twenties sat on the edge of the bed, tears dripping from her eyes onto the front of her pink, pleated dress. The woman stared down at the ground, as if too afraid to face what was in front of her. A calendar was displayed on the wall behind her. The month was too small to make out, but in big, bold letters, Addison could see the year: 1952.

The woman's eyes suddenly shifted, reacting to something or someone across from her. But the other side of the room remained hidden, shrouded from Addison's view. And sight wasn't the only sense Addison was missing: the room was devoid of all sound.

Addison approached the girl, bending down in front of her. "Are you all right? What's wrong?"

The girl didn't flinch, her petrified gaze still fixed on the other side of the room. She stared past Addison like she wasn't even there. Addison put her hand out to touch her, but yanked it back when a high-pitched noise pierced the silence. Sound rushed back into the room. The girl stood up and screamed, stretching both of her arms out in front of her, as if trying to push someone away.

"Please, don't," the girl begged. "Can't we talk about—"

The girl stopped, mid-sentence, her head slanted, eyes wide. She appeared to be listening, but how was that possible? No one else was there besides the two of them. Were they? The girl crisscrossed her hands, wrapping them over her stomach. Her entire body trembled like she was experiencing some kind of epileptic seizure. She glanced up, desperately pleading for her life. "No—no! What are you doing?! Stop!" she shrieked. "Don't do this—please!"

They were the last words the girl would utter.

A gun appeared in midair, hovering in front of the woman, but Addison's vision was clouded, shielding her from the identity of the person holding it. The woman reached out, clawing at the gun. Addison sprung forward, grabbing for it herself, but she missed. At least, she thought she did until she turned around and tried again. The second time, she watched her hand as it swept right through the gun, like it was made of air. She brought her hand down in front of her face, fingers stretched, and then tightened it into a ball. Her hand was solid, its warmth pulsating through her veins. So why couldn't she grab it? Addison turned once more; this time it was too late. A gunshot went off. Addison looked around. The woman was nowhere to be found. *Had she been shot? Where was she?* Moments later another shot rang out. The woman reappeared a few feet away from where Addison was standing. She looked past Addison and then her body sagged to the floor, lifeless. Blood oozed from her chest, filling cracks and crevices, saturating the wood floor in dark-red liquid.

Addison released the dress, allowing it to slump back inside the box. Light filtered into the room and she leaned forward, bracing a hand on the floor in front of her. She tried to suck in a breath or two but struggled to ingest even the tiniest amount of air.

It was happening—again.

CHAPTER 8

When Addison was a child, she saw things all the other "normal" kids didn't. Things no one ever talked about if they did. Things that made the people around her uncomfortable when *she* did. At age five, she'd attended a birthday for her friend, Natalie. As they ran around playing an innocent game of hide and seek in the backyard, Natalie's hair ribbon had fallen out. Addison found it. As soon as she bent down to pick it up the yard around her shifted into a haze of dark, misty fog. When the fog lifted, Natalie was no longer running in the yard. She was swinging on the tree swing. Addison waved and called out, but Natalie ignored her, not even glancing in her direction. Natalie pumped her legs faster and glared at her brother, who stared upward, taunting her, saying she could touch the sky and she still wouldn't ever be able to swing as high as he could. She made a face like she'd show him. She could do *anything* better than he could. Natalie stretched her legs all the way back and then kicked back as hard as she could, soaring upward until she was almost level with the branch the tree swing hung from. She curved her body forward to see if her brother was watching and squealed with victorious excitement when she saw that he was. She shouted something at him, not realizing that her body was tipped too far forward. She slipped, her hands desperately grappling at the rope on both sides of the swing to keep her from falling down. Her desperate attempt to save herself failed; the rope snapped and she fell several feet before smacking her head on one of the rock-like stepping stones that lined her mother's koi pond.

Addison scrambled to the side of her friend. "Natalie, wake up!" Natalie's eyes didn't open. Her brother stared down at his sister in a daze, not believing what had happened. "Get your parents!" Addison screamed. "Now!" But he didn't move. He just stood there. Addison ran inside the house. Her parents were sitting around the table playing cards together. "Hurry, come quick! Natalie fell. She won't wake up." But Natalie's mom just smiled at her husband and played the eight of hearts. "You have to do something!" Addison screamed. No one moved. No one looked at her. It was as if they didn't care.

Why aren't they listening to me?!

A few seconds later, Natalie's brother ran through the door. "Mom! Dad! Come quick. Natalie fell off the swing!"

Both parents shot up in unison. Natalie's mother's chair flipped on its side, slamming against the tile on the floor in the process. As mother, father, and son raced toward Natalie, Addison followed. Her mother screamed, her father dialed 9-1-1, and her brother leaned against the tree and cried. Then everything went black.

***

Addison woke to find several parents hovering over her.

"Are you all right, sweetheart?" one of the men said.

"I think so," Addison replied. "What happened?"

"We're not sure. We think you passed out. Are you feeling okay?"

"I—I think so. Where's Natalie?"

"She's in the house," the man said. "It's just about time to open presents. Why don't you come inside and we'll get you some water?"

"So, she's okay?"

"Natalie?"

Addison nodded.

"Of course she is," the man said.

"She didn't get hurt when she fell off the swing?"

"What swing?"

Addison pointed to it and only then noticed something strange—it had been tied to the side of the tree.

"No one's been on that swing at all today," the man said.

"But I saw her," Addison insisted. "She fell and hit her head on a stone by the pond."

The parents looked at each other in disbelief. The man held out his hand and Addison took it. Nothing else was said as they walked back into the house.

"Have you been on the swing today?" Addison said as soon as she saw Natalie.

"No."

"Good. Stay off of it," Addison said.

Natalie wrinkled her nose and frowned. "Why?"

"Because you—well—you could get hurt. The rope it was made out of—it isn't as strong as you think."

Natalie tossed her head back and laughed. "You're so silly, Addison. Wanna help me open my presents?"

Addison wanted to grab Natalie's arm. She wanted to tell her what she saw. But she didn't want to be laughed at again, so she fabricated a slight smile as she followed Natalie into the living room and tried her best to blend in with all of the other kids.

The adults were all huddled together in the corner talking when the girls walked in. One of the women in the group pinched the arm of the man standing next to her and simultaneously they looked over. All eyes were fixed on Addison, their grins a mere facade. Addison smiled back even though she knew what they were thinking: *That friend of Natalie's has something wrong with her. Something very wrong.*

***

Four months later, Natalie wasn't just hurt when she crashed to the ground while her stunned brother looked on. She was killed, in the exact same way Addison had seen in her vision. When Addison wasn't at school, she stayed in her bedroom for hours at a time, curled up in a ball on her bed, weeping. No one, not even her own mother, had believed her story. Her mother just hugged her, saying everything was going to be all right and she needn't worry. But nothing was all right, and it never would be. Natalie was dead and Addison heaped a great deal of the blame onto herself, always thinking there was something she might have done to prevent the inevitable from happening.

Over the next year, Addison received another vision, and then another. Most of the time the person was someone unfamiliar, someone she'd never seen before. While walking outside the city mall with her mother one day, she'd found a penny on the sidewalk. As soon as she smoothed a finger across its metallic surface, she saw a man peeking through a restaurant window. He was shivering, his arms covering his face, shielding him from the cold. He had no coat and no place to go. He just stood there, staring at the soft glow of the fire inside the place as if wishing he could be sitting beside it. Several weeks later, she saw his face again. This time it was on the news. The reporter said the man had been a transient, poor and homeless. The reporter also said the man was dead, his body found covered in newspaper on a bench at the local park. He'd been trying to keep warm, but it was an especially cold winter that year.

Addison thought about talking to her parents again, but she couldn't; she was too afraid. Instead, she became withdrawn, rarely speaking and lacking the interests other children had at her age. Her parents assumed she hadn't been able to get over Natalie's death and decided the answer to their problems was taking Addison to see a therapist named Doctor Arnold W. Beatty III. He counseled her mother not to "enable" Addison in any way. Translation: convince Addison that what she saw at Natalie's house wasn't real, even though in the end, the inevitable *had* happened. Though he had no explanation as to why Addison said she saw what she did, he was a firm believer that no one except God Himself could predict another individual's destiny. It just wasn't possible, and all the "quacks" who thought it was were just that—crazy people. The doctor had cautioned her parents that if they couldn't help her snap out of it, eventually she'd be ridiculed and made fun of at school for her unsocial, awkward behavior.

Addison despised Doctor Beatty, who she called "Doctor Death" because to her, he appeared old and decrepit. She also despised the constant stream of questions he asked, so after her third appointment, she did something she'd been taught never to do—she lied. She admitted to her mother and father that the day of the party she had made everything up. When she saw the tree swing in the yard, she imagined what would happen if someone ever fell from it. Her mother was satisfied enough to allow Addison to stop seeing Doctor Death and eventually Addison's visions faded so much, she herself stopped believing. Once that happened, the visions stopped coming. By the time she was eighteen, the memories of her early childhood were so vague, she wondered if they had ever been real at all.

Now, sitting in the room staring at the dress puddled inside the dress box, every memory she'd ever had rushed back to her like the gust of wind that swept Dorothy all the way to Oz. And the worst part of all? She hardly knew what to do about it.

CHAPTER 9

"You get the answers you were looking for?" Luke said, leaning against the doorway.

Addison was sitting on the ground, her legs crossed over one another, contemplating what had just happened. "Someone died here."

"What?"

Addison glanced upward, catching a brief glimpse of the effect her words had on Luke's face. "I'm sorry—I don't know what I'm talking about. I was thinking of something else when you walked in, and I just blurted out the first thing that came to mind."

He eyed her suspiciously. "You looked like you knew exactly what you were saying when you said it. What's that then?" he said, pointing at the dress.

She set the lid on top of the box. "It's nothing."

"Doesn't look like nothing."

"I found it in a box at the bottom of the trunk." She

pushed the lid to the side, just enough to allow a small piece of the fabric to dangle over the edge. "It's just some old party dress."

"What's all over it?" Luke asked.

"A design of some kind, I guess."

Addison tried covering the dress without touching it, but Luke knelt down, pushing the lid to the side, and pointing. "That doesn't look like any design I've ever seen."

"What does it look like to you?"

"Honestly? Dried blood," Luke said.

"Maybe. Or something was spilled on it. It could be a lot of different things."

"Like what?"

Nothing came to mind.

"Who would go to the trouble of boxing up a dress without cleaning it first?" He tugged at the edge of his chin. "Is that why you said someone had died here?"

"I told you—I don't know why I said that."

Luke stood. "If you don't want to tell me, fine. But don't lie to me."

"I'm not."

He slid a hand down his face and groaned. "I'm done for tonight. See you tomorrow."

He'd made it out the door and almost to his truck before Addison caught up with him. "Wait."

He kept walking.

"Would you wait just a minute?!" she yelled. "Please?"

He stopped, but didn't turn around. "Why?"

"You're right. I wasn't honest with you before, but believe me, it's better this way."

"How do you know?"

"If I shared certain things with you, you'd never see me the same way again. You'd think...I was crazy."

He shrugged. "You seem normal to me."

"Right now I do."

"All right. Tell me something...see what happens."

"And risk you leaving and not coming back?"

Luke faced her. "It's not going to happen, Addison. We've become friends over the past few weeks, haven't we?"

"I'd consider us friends, yes."

He sighed. "Then don't be afraid to let me into your life. I'm completely open. You can ask me anything, and I'll always give you a straight answer. You can tell me anything, and I won't judge you."

Even standing there, listening to his words, she didn't believe a person like him actually existed. "It's not that easy."

"Sure it is," he said. "There's no need to be shy, not around me."

Shy? Is that how he sees me?

"Are you happy?" he asked.

"What do you mean?"

He dug his hands into his pockets. "It just seems like you've built a wall around yourself."

"What do you mean?"

"You know. Just one brick—that's all I'm asking," he said, holding a finger in the air. "Tell me one thing you thought you couldn't ever tell anyone."

The Great Wall of Addison was created at a time in her life when trust should have been forming, not row upon row of bricks. But seeing things others didn't want to accept had taught her the value of keeping things to herself. As she aged, so did the need to separate herself from everyone else. Her introverted, untrusting nature came with a price, often at the expense of her relationships with men. None of them had ever lasted longer than six months, and usually, it was even less. They tried to get close, but she resisted, never trusting them enough to let herself go—not completely. She firmly believed that if she ever showed her true self, they'd laugh, and then they'd leave.

Luke was giving her the chance to do something different. She desperately wanted to keep the promise she'd made to herself to become a new, improved Addison, the one she'd always wanted to be. She just wasn't sure who that was yet. She looked at Luke, contemplating the next course of action and whether what she was about to say would haunt her forever. All he wanted was a single brick, but he was about to get a good bit of the wall. "Do you believe in spirits?"

CHAPTER 10

"You mean ghosts?" Luke asked.

"They're the same thing, aren't they?"

"Why do you ask?"

"You said you wanted a brick."

He looked at her like he didn't understand how the two were related and then walked over to the porch. "I shouldn't have pushed you just now. I'm sorry."

"It's fine—really," she said.

"Here I am asking you to do what I haven't even done myself. I want to share something with you, if you don't mind. Can we sit?"

He sat down, and Addison joined him.

"When I was twelve years old, my grandfather died," Luke said.

"Were you close?"

"Very. He used to pick me up on the weekends and take me to the renovation jobs he was working on."

"Is that why you went into the business—because of him?"

He nodded. "No matter what went wrong, my grandfather never complained. He just looked at me and said it would all work out. It drove me crazy at first. I thought he never took anything seriously. Then I watched things happen around him—a client would complain about the way something was done, or how much time he was taking to complete the job. It didn't faze him. He just went about his day, smiling and looking forward to the next day and the next one after that."

"Sounds like a smart man."

"He was—but he was so much more," Luke said. "When I was with him, I always felt special, like I was his favorite, and maybe I was. Now I get the feeling my cousins felt the same way too. My grandpa could have had one hundred grandchildren; it didn't matter. He had a way of making you feel like you were the only person who mattered."

The closest thing Addison had like that in her own life was her father, though the bond didn't seem as tight as the one Luke had just mentioned. "It must have been hard when you lost him."

"I wasn't prepared when it happened," he said. "I don't think anyone is, no matter the circumstances. I knew he was getting old; I just always thought I'd have more time."

Addison frowned. "I felt the same way about my mom."

"On the day of the funeral, I remember standing with my parents in a long line, waiting to pay our last respects. The closer we got to the casket, the more I didn't want to be anywhere near it. There were seven or eight people in front of us, but I could see my grandfather's head from where I was standing. It had been propped up high enough on the pillow that I could see him lying there. His eyes were closed, and his hands were placed one over the other in the middle of his body. He looked like he was dreaming, not dead. I wanted to shake him and wake him up—make him come back to me."

Addison winced. "Funerals were hard for me as a kid too."

"When we got closer to his casket, my mother turned to me and said, 'When it's our turn you can give him a kiss goodbye if you want.' I was a scared kid—I'd never even been around a dead person before. A kiss goodbye? I had this mental picture of me leaning in, my lips puckered, and when I was an inch or so from his cheek, his eyes would suddenly burst open, but instead of the soft blue I remembered, they'd be a whitish-grey color. And I'd realize the man staring back at me wasn't my grandfather anymore. I stood there going over and over it in my mind until my mom looked at me and said, 'Are you all right?' I broke from the line and bolted for the door."

"You left?" Addison asked.

"Before I got to the door my mother yelled my name. I turned and saw her step toward me, but my dad reached out and wound his fingers around her arm, reeling her back. He said, 'Let him go.' I thrust the church doors open and ran as fast as I could for as long as I could until I was so far away, I couldn't see the church anymore. I never turned back, I just kept on running. I made it a few blocks before my legs felt like they'd been dipped in cement blocks, and I couldn't run anymore. I collapsed on the grass in someone's front yard. I didn't know whose it was, and I didn't care. I didn't want to be alive anymore. Not without him."

Addison rested a hand on Luke's knee. "What an awful thing to go through."

Although Luke smiled, she noticed a sting of sadness in his eyes. They both remained stationary, neither moving, until Luke cleared his throat, producing a sound like he was trying to get rid of the knot in it.

"That night my parents tried to think of something they could do to cheer me up," he said. "I heard my mom tell my dad that she thought they should have a talk with me to help me 'process my feelings.' My dad said he had a much better idea."

"What did they come up with?"

"Ice cream," he said.

"Not bad."

"My stomach was so sour, I knew I'd never be able to eat it, but they were worried about me so I went along with it anyway. It made my mom relax a little. She probably thought I was feeling better about the whole thing."

"So what happened?" Addison asked.

"It was dark outside when we left the house. I was sitting in the middle of the back-seat of the car. My parents were in the front, laughing about silly things my grandpa had done or said. It was their attempt to loosen the mood. They probably thought it would help me in some way. It didn't. I sat there, feeling guilty for running out of the church and never saying goodbye. I wondered if my grandfather was out there somewhere, looking down on me, disappointed in the way I'd acted. He'd meant so much to me in life, and I couldn't even tell him that in the end."

"I'm sure he knew. I don't know where people end up after this life, but I'd like to believe they know how we feel."

Luke buried his head in his hands.

"What is it?" Addison asked.

"When my parents stopped talking and it was completely quiet inside the car, I thought I heard something."

"What was it?"

"A male voice."

Addison tried her best to remain calm and unchanged by his revelation. "What did the voice say?"

"It was low, like a whisper. Someone said, 'Luke.' The sound was so close to my face, I could feel a warm breath against my skin. I was terrified—my entire body went stiff. I tried to turn my head. I couldn't move."

"What about your parents? What did they do when it happened?"

"They just sat there," he said. "Obviously, they hadn't heard anything. For a few minutes, it was quiet, and then I heard the voice again. This time I could tell it was the voice of a man. He said, 'Luke, don't worry. It will all work out.'"

Addison clamped a hand over her mouth.

"I knew as soon as I heard it that it was my grandfather. It had to be. But how? I wanted to turn my head and look over to see if he was sitting on the seat next to me, but I couldn't—I just couldn't."

"So what did you do?"

"I covered my face with my hands and waited for it to get quiet again. Then, when it was, one by one I separated my fingers just wide enough to see about a foot in front of me."

"Did you see anything?"

"Yeah, a head," he said.

"A what?"

"My grandfather's head, floating in front of me, like some kind of a hologram formed by tiny particles of air. I could see the dashboard of my father's car right through it."

"His body wasn't attached?"

"I know it sounds crazy," he said.

"Not as crazy as you think. Did you ever try to talk to him?"

"I just sat there, staring at his head. He smiled at me, the way he always did, and then laughed and said, 'You'll be okay. Great things are coming your way, Luke. You'll see.' He told me he'd always be with me, and that he understood why I couldn't say goodbye earlier that day. Somehow I was able to nod at him, and once I did, he was gone."

"All of that while your parents sat in the front seat?"

"I know—I witnessed it, and I can hardly believe it myself. Because I was so young, it would be easy to look back on it now and convince myself that I'd made it all up, but I know what I saw."

"I believe you," Addison blurted out.

He turned toward her, astonished. "You do—why?"

She bobbed her shoulders up and down. "Why not? Who am I to say that what you saw wasn't real?"

Luke leaned back, his eyes never leaving her face. "There's something about you. You're so…different."

"Compared to what?"

"Other women."

"Trust me when I say—you don't know the half of it."

He leaned forward and placed his hand over hers. "I'd like to…get to know you, I mean."

Was it possible? Had she finally found someone she could open up to?

"I'm curious," she said. "Did you tell your parents what you saw that night?"

"I lay in bed all night thinking about it. I decided not to say anything, but the next morning, it was all I could think about it. My mom could tell something was weighing on me. She asked what it was, and I told her."

"And she didn't believe you, right?" she asked. "She probably thought you made the whole thing up."

"Why would you assume that?"

"I—I don't know."

"Actually, she took my dad aside and told him what I'd said. Then they came into my room, and we all discussed it together."

"Did they send you to counseling?"

He raised a brow. "Counseling? I don't understand."

"Wait—are you saying they believed you?" she asked.

"Why wouldn't they?"

"Because they were in the car when it happened and

neither of them saw or heard anything."

"My mother didn't need to experience it to believe me. She's always been a woman of great faith. She was overjoyed. She said my grandfather chose me because I was special and that she felt a lot better knowing he would be watching out for me. My father went to the store and bought me a journal. He said to write every detail of the experience down so I'd never forget it, but I didn't need to write it down. I knew I would never forget."

Addison looked away. "You're lucky—most parents wouldn't see it that way." Her phone vibrated inside of her pants pocket. She took it out and read the text message: CAN'T WAIT TO SEE YOU TONIGHT, HONEY. DAD. "I'm sorry, I have to go. My father is flying in at six and we're meeting in the city for dinner."

"Will I get the chance to meet him?"

"I don't think so—he has a meeting in the morning. He's flying back out tonight."

He stood. "Maybe some other time. Listen, thank you for listening to my story."

"It means a lot that you felt comfortable enough to share it with me," she said.

"I do…feel comfortable," he said, "but there's one thing I don't understand."

"What's that?"

"How is it that you believed me so easily? Most

people wouldn't."

Luke's loaded question was something she wasn't prepared to answer, so she made an excuse about not having enough time to get ready before meeting with her father and said they'd talk again later. He gave her a look to indicate his disappointment and said he hoped they could revisit the subject again the next morning.

The more Addison thought about what had been happening since she arrived at Grayson Manor, the more curious she was about remembering the visions she'd had as a child. Had it been some kind of gift? It felt more like a curse. She didn't want it, and she hadn't asked for it. She didn't even know where it came from or why. She wondered if there were others in the world like her. More than anything, she just wanted someone to make sense of it all—someone to tell her what she was meant to do, or if she was to do nothing? If that was the case, what was the point of receiving the visions at all? Did she have a role, a part to play? If so, what was it? And why hadn't she experienced anything else for so many years? Why now?

CHAPTER 11

David Lockhart sat outside of the Bella Italia restaurant on an uncomfortable iron bench and waited. His daughter, Addy, was already ten minutes late. This fact didn't surprise him in the least. She was frequently late. In fact, he couldn't recall her ever arriving on time for anything in her life.

He shoved a hand in his pocket, running his fingers over an envelope he'd received in the mail a week earlier. He'd debated the contents of the letter for several days, not knowing whether it was time to come clean and reveal the truth to Addy or if he should honor the agreement he'd made with his wife to never speak of it. The decision wasn't an easy one, and he'd wrestled with it on several occasions over the last few days. No matter what he decided, there would be consequences, of this he was sure. What he wasn't sure of was which one he could live with. He'd never fully agreed with his wife's decision to keep things from Addy, but as long as she'd been alive, he went along with it anyway. It made her happy, and he liked keeping people happy.

David had kept in touch with Addy every day since his wife's death, always worrying about her decision to seclude herself in a new place where she had no friends and no family. He believed it was temporary and that she was just running away. Once she had time to adjust to her mother's death, he hoped she'd return home where she belonged. His wife's death had skewered him like the pointy tip of a bull's horn, leaving a permanent scar on his heart, a constant reminder that wouldn't ever go away—not completely.

Over the past weeks, he'd pondered a lot about his life, taking heed of the not-so-gentle reminder that things can change at any time. His beautiful, loving wife was gone, and he was left to face life alone, without her. He hadn't been ready.

From a parking lot across the street, Addy came into view. He practically leapt off the bench and rushed over to greet her. "I'm so happy to see you, Addy." He clutched her with both hands, pulling her into his chest.

"Dad, I've really missed you." Tears gathered in her eyes. "Are you doing all right?"

He draped an arm around her, and they walked into the restaurant. "Better. I drop by the cemetery and visit your mother's grave on my way home from work each day. Probably seems like a silly thing to do, but telling her about my day keeps her with me somehow."

"If it makes you feel better, I think you should visit Mom as much as you need to. One day, you'll be able to let go. It doesn't have to be today."

It had been a few short weeks since he'd seen his daughter, but she looked different somehow, older, as if she'd aged a few years in a matter of weeks. Dark circles masked her tired eyes. He wanted to take her back with him, take her home, look after her. But he knew she would never allow that. She'd do her best to convince him she was strong and not the dwindling flame standing before him.

They were led to a booth and seated.

"So, do you like it here?" he asked.

"I'm glad I'm out of the city."

"How's the house?"

She paused several seconds before responding.

"Different than what I thought it would be."

"How so?" he asked.

"Have you ever been to the manor before?"

"No, why?"

"When I told you it had been left to me in mom's will, you were startled."

"I'll admit it. I was. I mean, I knew it existed, but your mother hated living in that house."

Her face tightened. "Do you know why?"

"All I know is that she felt it was filled with bad memories."

"But she was so young when she left there. It's hard for me to believe she remembered much of anything."

"How did you know she moved away as a child?" he asked.

"The neighbor, a Helen something. She never actually told me her last name when we met. She said she used to watch Mom sometimes when she was a child."

Her father stiffened; his gaze shifting from her to the napkin in front of him. "Your mother didn't like talking about her childhood much. I only know that when her father left, she blamed her mother for everything—for the divorce, for taking her away from her friends, and for all the moving around they did. Her life was never the same after that. Marjorie moved them from town to town, always making the same promise—that this time they'd settle down. Then your mother would return home after a day at school and she'd find their bags packed and the car running."

"No wonder they didn't have a good relationship. Did you know her?"

"Marjorie?" he asked.

She nodded.

"We met briefly," he said. "She came to our wedding. Tried to give your mother her wedding ring. She wouldn't take it. Marjorie begged her; she said she'd do anything to start over again and make things right. But your mother—well, she didn't want any part of it, and I couldn't blame her."

"Did Mom ever look for her father?"

"No. I even suggested it to her once, saying I'd hire a private investigator. I figured after you were born, she might be open to the idea. She wasn't."

The waiter delivered the food and they spent the next several minutes in silence. The look of longing and loss in Addy's eyes mimicked his own. It troubled him to see her in so much pain. She tried to hide it with a slight grin and an upbeat tone, but he wasn't convinced. She twisted several noodles around her fork and then released them, watching them spill back onto the plate. "Addy, are you sure you're all right? What's troubling you?"

She cleared her throat, sat up, and looked at him. "I need to ask you something."

"Anything."

"Do you remember Natalie?"

David's face felt cold and clammy like he'd just been stuck in a freezer. He set down his fork, wiped his mouth with a napkin, and laced his fingers together on top of the table. "I wondered if this would ever get brought up again. Why now?"

"I've been thinking about her a lot lately."

"Maybe your mother's accident elicited feelings you haven't thought about in a long time. Could that be it?"

"After I told Mom what I saw the day I was at Natalie's house, she asked me never to talk about it again. Do you remember?"

Of course he remembered. "We were just worried about you."

"It was more than that—you didn't believe me, Dad. Neither one of you did."

He reached across the table, placing a hand on top of hers. "Who says I didn't?"

"The two of you put me in counseling. If that doesn't scream 'non-believer,' I don't know what does."

"We never meant to disregard your feelings, honey. I'm sure they were very real at the time. I still remember the look on your face when you told me. You were so certain. And then it happened. Natalie fell from the swing to her death. I didn't know what to think. Truth is, it scared me, and I could tell it scared you too. I didn't want you to go through life like that."

"So you ignored it?"

Her father glanced to the side, speaking to the air. "I'll never forget the day I got the phone call from Natalie's parents. I didn't want to believe it was true."

"Didn't it make you wonder how I was able to predict something *before* it ever happened?"

"When you fainted at the birthday party, I'd believed

for a brief moment you were granted the ability to see into the future, but that was a fluke, like some kind of a dream or a premonition. I didn't want you dwelling on the death of that little girl for the rest of your life."

"Is that why you made me shut it out? Did you ever think that if something had been done—like the tree swing had been removed—Natalie might be alive today?"

"When it's your time to go, it's your time," he said. "Death would have come some other way…if not from the swing, maybe a sickness of some kind. You can't cheat death."

"I don't believe you. It was a warning. I could have helped her."

He leaned forward. "Honey, neither of us knows why you saw what you did. Your mother and I made a decision to put you in counseling so that you could move on from what happened. So you could be a kid. Besides, you never saw anything after that."

"How do you know?"

"Because you would have mentioned it to us," he said.

"After what I was put through, why would I?"

He released her hand. *It couldn't be true, could it?* "What are you saying?"

"Natalie wasn't the only vision I ever had. There were others."

David slid his hand back in his pocket again,

running the thin paper through his fingers. Was it time? He was unsure. "Did you tell anyone about the other things you saw?"

She hung her head, staring into the napkin folded over her lap. "I knew no one would believe me if I did."

"Oh, Addy. How long has this been going on? How many times?"

"After Natalie died, there were visions of other people I'd never seen before. They all came one right after the other."

"How long did this go on?" he asked.

"When I started seeing the counselor, it all stopped."

"He obviously helped you in some way."

But he knew better. Counseling hadn't helped her, it had hurt her, and he was to blame. He'd already lost his wife. He wasn't ready to lose his daughter too. He released the letter back into his pocket, tucked safely away. Revealing its contents would have to wait.

After dinner they walked in silence back to her car. There was so much more he wanted to say, but somehow couldn't find the right way to say it. She unlocked the door, leaned over, and kissed her father on the cheek. "I love you, Dad. I'll call you tomorrow, okay?"

CHAPTER 12

Addison's drive home was filled with haunted memories of the time she'd spent in a dimly lit room under the watchful, hawk-like eye of Doctor Death. Back then, his mere presence stifled her, producing a lasting effect that had removed her visions altogether. And as much as she loved her father, the thought that he had sent her to that doctor pained her to this day. She shook her head back and forth trying to shake the unwelcome memories away and shift the focus to the here and now. Presently, the here and now was sitting on the top step of the front porch looking forlorn.

"What are you doing here, Luke? I thought you'd be gone by now."

"I wanted to make sure you made it home okay. Besides, you said your father was going back home tonight, so I didn't think it would bother you if I came back and finished up a couple things."

She nudged past him and looked around. "What *things?* The house looks the same way it did when I left. What couldn't wait until tomorrow?"

He walked up behind her. "I'm going to tell you something. Promise me you won't be mad, okay?"

His face, the perfect combination of guilt and concern, was easy to read. Still, she didn't know what he could have done to cause anger to swell within her. And then came a moment of complete clarity and somehow she just knew. Addison crossed the room, flinging open the door to the room at the end of the hall. Her eyes darted around, searching for the white box. It was gone.

"I was waiting for you to come home so we could talk about this." Luke entered the room, box in hand.

"Give that to me!" She snatched the closed box from his hands.

"Look, I'm sorry, okay? I know I didn't have any right—"

"I want you to leave."

"Addison, if I could just—"

"Get out!" she said, pointing.

"I really am sorry," he said, walking away.

Addison froze. "Did you touch it?"

Luke turned. "I just handed it back to you, so you know I did."

"Not the box—the dress. Did you touch the dress?"

He nodded.

"And?" she asked.

"And what?"

She didn't know how to respond.

"Addison, what is going on?"

"Nothing. It doesn't concern you."

He kept walking. "Fine."

She rushed after him. "You come into *my* house, open something that belongs to *me*, and *I'm* the one to blame?"

He pointed at the box. "I knew those were blood stains earlier."

"So there's a little blood on it. So what—who cares?"

"It's not a small amount of blood, Addison."

"The dress is decades old. I don't even know who owned it or why it's here."

"Open the box," he demanded.

"What—no, I won't."

"Why?"

"It doesn't matter."

"When I took it out and looked at it, I thought someone might have died in that dress," he said. "But I don't think so now."

She wanted to ignore his insinuation—act like she didn't care, even though she did. "What changed your mind?"

"I turned it inside out. Some of the stains don't go all the way through."

"Your point?"

"It's someone else's blood," he said.

"Like I said, the dress is old."

"Yeah, but aren't you curious?"

"I don't want to talk about this anymore."

The front door slammed to a close. Apparently, neither did he.

CHAPTER 13

Addison sat on the bed, the box resting in between her legs. She ran her fingers over the lid, then hesitated and recoiled, sagging into the pillow behind her. She thought about punting the box across the room, the lid flying open, and the dress spilling out all over the floor. *What will happen if I touch it again? Will it be different this time?* She clutched the sides of the box, setting it down on the floor beside her. Maybe tomorrow, while Luke worked in a different area of the house, she'd be brave enough to try again.

Sleep came minutes later, relieving her of the exhaustion she had felt the night before. The hours ticked by in silence, until the clock on her bedside table struck four. A frigid air stirred her from sleep. She reached down, tugging on the covers, but bringing them up past her chin made no difference; the temperature in the room had plummeted so that she felt the chill of her breath resting on her cheeks.

Her eyes flashed open. A faint light, in the shape of a misty, white figure, faded in and out. It was soft at first, offering a pale illumination to the room. Steam from her breath floated into the open air and then dissipated in front of her as she continued to breathe in and out. She was in too much shock to notice. The shape shifted inside the light like a baby animal struggling to break free from the hardened shell that confined it.

Addison sat straight up in bed, terror gripping her body. The light moved closer. It lingered at the edge of the bed, bobbing up and down for a few seconds before it stopped. Long, skeletal fingers punctured a hole in the light, reaching out and gently wrapping bony digits around the bed's iron railing. Addison's screams echoed throughout the house as the light separated, and from it, a silhouette emerged—the same sad, scared young woman Addison had seen hunched in the corner in her vision the day before. The woman wore the same pleated dress, except this time, a large portion of it was stained with blood. The blood on the dress was dry, like it had been stuck there for years, fusing together with the fabric surrounding it.

The woman stared at Addison, never blinking, the look on her spectral face a mixture of heartbreak and longing. She didn't speak. She just hovered there as if waiting for something. But what? Addison had never interacted with anyone in her visions before. When she'd called out to the Natalie of the future, her cries went unheard. The woman was from the past, but appeared before Addison in the present. Would it make a difference?

Filled with a newfound confidence, Addison met the ghostly gaze. The woman meant no harm. She was sure of it. She had to be. "What's your name?"

The woman's head slanted to the side, but she didn't utter a word.

"Why are you here?" Addison pressured.

Again, no response.

"Did something happen to you in this house? Is that why you've returned?"

After failing for the third time, Addison mumbled, "Well, I guess *you* can't communicate with me either."

The woman's mouth opened a little and she uttered two words so faint, Addison barely heard them. "Help me."

Addison flinched, goose bumps lining the length of her arms. *Is this really happening?* "How can I help you?"

A tear seeped from the corner of the woman's eye. It trailed down her ashen cheek, dissolving once it was released into the air.

"Isn't there anything else you can tell me?" Addison asked. "Please. I don't know what to do."

"Help me," the woman pleaded, a second time. She released her hand from the bed post, sweeping an unstable finger through the air. Her finger steadied once it found its target and the movement stopped. Addison thought about glancing at the floor, but she didn't have to. She knew what she'd set there hours earlier. She understood. A subtle heat burned within her, the kind that filled one's life with meaningful purpose. She would find out everything she could about this woman: how she lived, how she died, and most importantly, who was responsible for ending her life.

The woman's lips parted again, and Addison remained still, poised and ready, but she wouldn't get what she was waiting for. Not this time. The glimmering light reappeared, and the woman closed her eyes, submitting herself to it. Tiny fragments chipped away at her frame, sucking her back into the light. And then she was gone.

CHAPTER 14

Addison tucked her knees under her chin, her arms folded around her legs. *How long have I been here? An hour? More?* Her body felt heavy, like a huge, petrified rock. Outside she could hear the sound of gravelly pebbles crunching beneath the tires of Luke's pickup truck. A minute later the front door opened and closed. Addison tried to stand. She couldn't.

"Addison, you up there?" Luke called.

"I'm…here."

"You decent?"

"Yes."

Luke entered her room saying, "Look, I'm sorry about what happened last night. I had no right to—"

Addison managed to partially lift a hand, stopping him. She tried to stand again, but her wobbly, spaghetti-like legs couldn't sustain her weight. "I…I want to tell…I see…I saw…"

Luke crossed the room, grabbing hold of her arm and lifting her back to the bed again. "Whoa, hang on a second. Why don't you sit back down first and catch your breath?"

She leaned back, masking her eyes with a quivering hand in the hopes he wouldn't notice the tears. He placed his hand over hers, gently pulling back.

"Are you sick?" he asked. "I can run to the store and get you some—"

"I see things," she croaked.

She glanced at him, fearing the same reaction she received as a child. His expression remained unchanged. He pulled the chair out from under a desk, flipped it around and sat down in front of her. "All right, what kinds of things?"

"You remember that brick you asked for?"

He nodded.

"This would be it. I just don't know if I—"

He squeezed her hand. "You can."

She blinked away the tears and began by relating the experiences she'd had as a child. She told him what happened sometimes when she touched things. She mentioned Natalie, her childhood friend, the man on the street, and other visions she'd experienced. Luke appeared concerned and convinced at the same time. When she finished, he smiled and rubbed her hand with his finger. "I knew there was something special about you, Addison Lockhart."

She'd told him about her past—a first step to seeing how he'd react before she told him about her present. And he'd accepted it without question, without judgment—something she'd never experienced in her life.

"I haven't even told you the best part yet," she said.

A look of excitement flashed across his eyes. "I'm ready. Shoot."

"What I'm about to say might sound a little crazy."

"Crazier than what you just told me?"

"This is…different."

"Whatever it is," he said. "You can tell me."

For the first time in a long time, there was no hesitation, just clarity. "I've experienced some weird things since I moved into this house."

He raised a brow. "Like what?"

"Well, the first night I slept here, I heard this noise. It sounded like a whiny cat. At least I thought it was a cat. Then it sounded more like a woman crying. I walked around, trying to identify it."

"Did you?"

She shook her head. "When I came back upstairs, I swore I saw the doorknob from the first bedroom on this floor light up."

"Like what?"

"Luke—it was glowing. I felt like I was being

beckoned toward it."

"What did you do?" he asked.

"We tried the door before. It's locked—remember? I was too afraid to touch it. I didn't want to admit what I was seeing was real. I feel so childish for saying this, but I went back to my room and ducked under the covers. Then everything stopped. I thought maybe it had all been a terrible dream until the next day when the visions I had as a kid came back."

"You had a vision?"

"Yes, when I touched the dress."

"The one in the trunk?"

Addison nodded. "There was a woman in a room. I couldn't tell where she was exactly, except that the walls looked familiar to me, like the ones in this house."

Although surprised, Luke retained his composure and kept quiet.

"She was shriveled up in a ball in the corner of the room begging for her life."

"Was anyone else there with her?" he asked.

"I could only see her at first. Then something else came into view, an object. A gun. It was aimed right at her."

Luke's eyes widened. "Was it in someone's hands? Did you see anyone?"

"Whoever was holding it was hidden from me. The gun just dangled in the air as if it defied gravity. I stared at it, fascinated, until two shots fired—killing her."

"Are you saying she was murdered? In this house?"

"I think it was here—I don't know. The only thing I'm sure of is that she wasn't from this time period. She wore a cocktail dress in a style not from this time."

"And you're sure you didn't see anything else?"

Addison shut her eyes, digging deep into her memory. "There was something. A calendar was tacked to the wall behind her."

"Did you see the month, the date, anything?"

She closed her eyes again, focusing on the lines and then the numbers. "The year was 1952. I'm almost positive."

He sat straight up, placing a hand over his chest like he was unable to draw breath. "Then she didn't die recently. It all makes sense. No wonder you were so angry when you found out I'd touched the dress."

"Whatever happened to the woman I saw, the dress has something to do with it, or I wouldn't have been able to see anything."

"Have you touched it since?"

"No—but I didn't have to. She came to me again last night. When I woke up she was standing at the edge of my bed. Well…not standing so much as hovering."

"Did she say anything?"

"Two words: help me."

"*Help me*," Luke muttered. "Hmm. I've always

believed in spirits. I don't know why they show themselves to some and not others, or why, but I believe when it does happen, whether they're good or evil, there's always a reason."

"I don't understand it…I haven't had a vision in years."

"Why do you think they stopped until now?"

She shrugged. "When my parents didn't believe me, I just tried to forget. I would have done anything to avoid seeing Doctor Death one more time."

"Doctor Death?"

"It was a silly name I called my therapist as a child."

"So to recap…when you had the vision of Natalie falling from the swing, you believed it."

"And it came true."

"You were a child," he said. "Children are desperate to believe in things. In a child's world, magic exists. Your parents held you back, sending you to the shrink to make you a nonbeliever."

"And it worked…sort of."

"I think when you stopped believing or shut it out, your ability was stripped from you somehow leading you to believe what you saw wasn't possible."

She felt like her head was spinning. "Do you think it made a difference?"

"Seems like most of the time believers see things others don't. Like those who refuse to accept what's right in front of them aren't gifted in the same way."

"But it's not like I moved into this house and started believing again. The vision just happened. I didn't solicit it."

"What if you being here solicited it? There's something tying you to this woman and this house. The place was passed down to you—if something happened here years ago, your connection might have triggered it, brought it back to life."

Addison removed the covers and swung her feet over the side of the bed. "Even if you're right, how am I supposed to help a dead woman? I don't even know who she is."

"Find out. You know the year. It shouldn't be hard for you to look it up and see if a young woman died around that time. Maybe she's been waiting for you all along."

CHAPTER 15

The *Rhinebeck Bee* was a small-scale newspaper established in 1930 during a time when money was tight and prohibition laws were even tighter. This fact, however, didn't stop the paper from churning out a couple of issues a month, a determination that kept it thriving eighty years later.

A brown-haired receptionist with paper-white skin and a starched shirt buttoned down so low anyone passing by could easily assess what a Wonderbra could do for an A cup, twisted a pen around her straight, shoulder-length hair. She didn't notice Addison come in. She didn't notice Addison approach the desk. She only noticed a giant of a boy with a camera slung around his neck that stood at her desk making ill-humored remarks. Addison cleared her throat but to no avail. The giggles were too loud.

"Oh, Kirk, you're so funny," the girl said. "You have

to stop distracting me. I have to get back to work."

"Doing what, Shelby? I haven't seen you do anything since I got here."

"That's because you keep pestering me," she said, lightly poking his leg with a pen.

"Just say the word, and I'll stop."

"What if I don't want you to?"

He flashed a devilish grin her direction and walked away.

"Excuse me," Addison said.

Shelby looked up. She wasn't smiling now. "Yeah?"

"Am I disturbing you?"

"No, why?"

"You are the receptionist, right?"

Shelby grabbed the coffee cup sitting next to her, slurped some of it down, and combed a hand through her hair like she was afraid one of the strands might be out of place. When the ritual was complete, she said, "Uh…yeah?"

"Who do I talk to about looking through some old newspapers?"

"What for?"

Addison clenched her hands into fists. This was the exact type of person she'd left Los Angeles to get away from. "Why do you need to know? Papers are public information, are they not?"

Shelby forced a smile. "Like, how old?"

Before Addison could answer, Giant Camera Boy leaned his head out of his office, looked her way, and smiled. Shelby craned her neck and turned as if a third eye in the back of her head made her magically aware of his presence.

"Look, you two can get a hotel later, but right now, I need some information."

Shelby's head snapped back into place. "What did you say?"

"You heard me."

"I'm married," the girl said, flashing a sparkly, yellow diamond on her ring finger.

"Then maybe you should start acting like it."

Shelby appeared too dumbfounded to respond. Tired of the girls' foolish games, Addison marched past her into the first office on the left. A man in a striped suit wearing a Tweety Bird tie eyeballed her and said, "If you need something, the receptionist is out front." He then attempted to wave Addison out of his office. In response, she sat down across from him, letting him know she'd gone that route already and she wasn't going to do it again. He listened to her request while watching the seconds tick by on the wall clock. When she finished, he hastily said it was true—they did keep back issues of every paper they'd ever published, but they were on a deadline at the moment. He wouldn't be able to let her back there, maybe for hours. Her best bet and her fastest one, he explained, was to visit the library in the city.

CHAPTER 16

Barry had enjoyed his position as manager of the biggest public library in New York City for the past thirty-four years. Years that had stripped him of his sportsman-like waistline, replacing it with a bowl full of fatty goo. His protruding tummy required the continual use of suspenders to ensure the top of his drawers never showed the public more than they bargained for. But he didn't mind. He'd grown fond of the suspenders over time, especially when he discovered they came in multiple colors. Patterned colors even. Today he was donning a pair of blue and white striped ones, a gift from his ailing mother.

***

Addison spotted Barry immediately, noting his suspenders had been hoisted up as high as they could go—a good two inches past his belly button. One would think it would have been the main attraction when looking at Barry, but even more prominent was the foam brace positioned around his neck.

"Excuse me?" Addison asked.

He swiveled around. "Yes?"

"Do you work here?"

Barry tapped the plastic name plate pinned over his right breast pocket.

"Can you tell me where I might find the newspaper archives?" she asked.

"Which ones?"

"I'd like to look at everything you have from the late fifties."

"I meant which paper," he said, with a wink.

"The *Rhinebeck Bee.*"

Barry inserted his thumbs beneath the suspenders, running them up and down. "Follow me."

Barry led her down a spiral staircase. He tried on occasion to glance to the side as he spoke, but his neck brace kept his head taut, as if hot glued in place.

"You one of those history buffs or somethin'?" Barry asked.

"No. I'm just trying to find information on someone."

"A relative?"

"I'm not sure—I don't think so."

"Whadd'ya expect to find if you don't know who you're looking for?" he joked.

She changed the subject. "Have you worked here long?"

"Long enough. I suppose I could retire. I don't relish the idea of sitting around the house with nothing to do except watch *Spenser: For Hire* reruns all day. Not that I wouldn't enjoy it. You ever see that show?"

She'd never even heard of it before. "I don't believe so."

"You should watch it sometime. Robert Urich was a damn good actor, you ask me. Died too young." Barry opened a door on the right and extended his hand, ushering Addison inside. "Okay, these boxes here on the third shelf," he pointed, "are labeled with the year on the front, so it's easier for you to find the one you want. The *Rhinebeck Bee* didn't publish as much as some of their larger counterparts, so there's only one box per year. Shouldn't be too hard for you to find what you need. I'll leave the door open—holler at me if you need anything else. Of course it might take some time for me to get back down here."

Addison smiled. "If I need anything, I'll come find you."

He walked out the door, hesitating before climbing the stairs to the main level. "I hope you find whatever it is you're looking for. The papers have all been preserved inside plastic sleeves, but they're the originals. Best you be gentle."

"I'll keep that in mind."

She pulled down a box labeled: *Rhinebeck Bee: 1952.* The first seven months' worth of papers didn't contain any information about a missing woman. It wasn't until she perused the paper for August that she found something—a headline which read: "Young Starlet Still Missing." She used the tips of her fingers to gently remove it from the box.

Dominating the center of the front page, in black and white, was a woman—smiling, vibrant, full of life and confidence—almost unrecognizable when compared to the frail, panic-stricken woman she'd seen over the past two days.

But it *was* her.

Addison was sure of it.

The woman was twenty-nine, the same age as Addison. Her raven-colored hair was long and lustrous. It parted in the middle of her forehead, falling into thick, loose curls over both sides of her face, nearly covering her eyes. She stood, legs spread wide, hands on hips, staring into the camera like she didn't just plan to live in the world, she planned to own it.

The date on the paper was August 25, 1952. The article read:

It has been two weeks since the disappearance of up-and-coming actress Roxanne "Roxy" Rafferty, Oscar-

nominated for her role in Joseph Lennart's film, *A Night in Paris*. Rafferty was last seen attending a dinner party in Rhinebeck, New York. When questioned, party host Marjorie Grayson said in a statement to police that the actress had left her home shortly after eleven that evening. She hadn't seen or heard from the Hollywood starlet since that time. Police have questioned everyone in attendance that night, but as of today, Rafferty's whereabouts are unknown. A thorough search of the actress's home has been conducted. At this time police have not commented about the search, divulged any new leads, or said whether foul play has been suspected.

Roxanne Rafferty, age twenty-nine, first starred in the critically-acclaimed romantic comedy, *Stolen Kisses*, at the tender age of twenty-one. Since that time, Rafferty has been highly sought after and widely regarded as an actress with the ability to bring success to any role she's given. Often seen playing the role of the beautiful and confident girl next door, it's been widely speculated that doe-eyed Rafferty was involved with her costars both on and off screen.

Three years ago, rumors circulated of her romance with actor Phillip Edwards while on the set of *Fly Me Away* and were quickly confirmed when Rafferty was seen donning a three-carat, diamond-and-platinum engagement ring, said to be given to her by the dashing actor, who was ten years her senior. But the wedding *never came to pass and was eventually called off by Rafferty soon after she started filming A Night in Paris, where she was believed to be dating another costar, this time leading-actor and already-married Hugh Brandon.*

The article went on to say that Rafferty's disappearance occurred at the same time Norman Grayson went missing, creating speculation that the two of them had left town together after the party at Grayson Manor. Witnesses from the night of the party gave conflicting reports, some saying Grayson and Rafferty were seen leaving together, others saying Rafferty left earlier while Grayson had remained.

Addison pulled a piece of scrap paper out of her wallet and a miniature-sized pencil she'd snagged from a desk upstairs and jotted down anything she felt was relevant information. She snapped a few photos with her camera phone and then forwarded them to Luke. Then she carefully slipped the newspaper back into place and searched the rest of that year for any further information on the missing woman.

There was none.

Addison returned the box to the shelf and retrieved the one for the following year. The second article she found was headlined: "Where Is Roxanne Rafferty?" In the article, it was reported that no new leads had surfaced over the past six months. Police were baffled, speculating that she was indeed dead, although her body had never been found. Some friends and family insisted Rafferty wouldn't just walk away from such a promising, lucrative career, including two starring roles slated to begin filming the following year.

There were no further articles on the disappearance of her grandfather, and a search of all the papers for the rest of 1953 turned up one additional result for Rafferty. A meager, insignificant article written on page six proclaimed the case had gone cold. Investigators shelved it, pending new leads. But there weren't any new leads—not that year, not the next year, and not the year after that. Everyone had moved on.

CHAPTER 17

Addison did not recognize the names Hugh Brandon or Phillip Edwards, and she was sure she'd never seen any of their movies. When she reminisced about famous names from the bygone era, Clark Gable, Cary Grant, and Gary Cooper came to mind, among others. But not these two names. Had something caused both Hugh and Phillip's stars to fade? Hollywood had a way of discarding people now and then, replacing them with younger, more robust and ambitious actors.

The fate of both men was only one of many on Addison's mind. She wondered how her grandparents were affiliated with the elite of society. Sure, her grandmother had looked the part, but her mother had said Marjorie was a working-class girl—not the next Marilyn Monroe. Had her mother lied? And what of her grandfather?

"You lost?" A woman in her late forties clasping the

rod to a yellow umbrella, even though it wasn't raining outside, squinted, staring quizzically into Addison's eyes. The moment the woman stopped, so did the little black dog she was walking. The dog sauntered over to the woman's side and sat on the pavement, as if he'd been given some kind of nonverbal cue. The woman smiled, clearly in awe of his talents. "Good boy, Reggie." She reached into her pocket and flicked a little red piece of meat, which the dog caught in his mouth before it had the chance to hit the ground.

"I'm sorry," Addison replied. "Was I in your way?"

"You didn't hear me say 'excuse me' a moment ago?"

Addison shook her head.

"Do you need help finding something?" the woman asked.

"I don't know."

The woman shrugged. "All right then. But you probably should watch where you're going. Most people around here aren't as polite as I am."

"Believe me," Addison said, "I know what it's like to live in the city."

The woman looped the dog leash around her hand a couple times and then gave it a gentle tug. "Walk on," she said. The dog moved forward in a straight line like a metal wind-up toy.

"Wait," Addison shouted.

The woman glanced halfway over her shoulder, her

body aligned on its current course. "What is it? Be quick. You're disrupting Reggie's routine."

"Do you know a place around here that sells old movies?"

The woman thought about it for exactly one second before huffing a sharp, "Nope, sorry." She then whipped her head back around, marching in a much brisker manner than before.

No further questions, your honor.

Addison leaned against the stucco exterior of a department-store building and sighed. She closed her eyes, trying to shut out all of the hustle and flow that came along with life in a big city.

What am I doing?

She was alone in her thoughts long before someone tugged on the sleeve of her jacket. It was light but insistent, like the gentle plea of a child. Only it wasn't. An elderly man, no more than five feet tall, smiled up at her with his one good eye while the lazy one seemingly stared at nothing. The plaid cap he wore on his patchy, thinning head made him look like a taxi cab driver, even though she sensed he wasn't one.

"I do," he said.

"I'm sorry?"

"You asked the dog lady if she knew where to find old movies. I do."

"All right, where?"

"Can you give me a ride?" he asked.

His tenuous body gave her little cause for concern. "Where do you need a ride to?"

"You want to buy old movies, don't you? I know a place."

"I don't have a car," Addison stated, deciding safety came first, no matter how innocent he seemed.

"Sure you do. It's the silver one over there," he said, a calloused finger bent in the right direction.

Her eyes widened. "How do you know that?"

"I watched you get out of it. You entered the library at half past twelve and came out five minutes before three."

"Are you following me?"

"I'm waiting," he said.

"For who?"

"My brother, Barry. He works there."

Barry confirmed that Raymond was just trying to secure a ride home. Occasionally he brought him along, leaving Raymond to sit at a table in one of the conference rooms and read while he worked. It was Barry's way of getting his brother out of the house. But Raymond lacked patience, often trying to procure a ride home from anyone he thought would give it to him. On occasion, he succeeded. Addison agreed to drop Raymond at home in exchange for him pointing out the location of the movie store.

Forty minutes and one drop-off later, she entered a tiny shop with heavy, black bars on the windows in a questionable part of town. The door should have jingled when she entered, given the strand of metal bells hanging from the handle. If it did, no one heard it. The sounds blaring through the oversized speakers mounted on the wall made sure of that.

"'Sup?"

Addison turned to face a man with piercings in his nose, ears, tongue, and on his forehead, though how that was possible, she didn't know.

"I'm Alex," he said, his body bouncing up and down to the rhythmic beat as he spoke. "You're cute—like in a hot kind of way."

"I think I'm in the wrong place," she said, taking a step backward.

"Looks right to me," he winked. "Funny how the sweet-looking babes all like the hard stuff."

Does he mean drugs? Or the music? Or both?

She turned to leave. He tapped her on the shoulder.

"Seriously, what are you looking for?"

"I was told I could find old movies here. I was told wrong. Sorry."

Addison pushed the door open.

"Hang on," he said.

The music switched off, leaving Addison with one thought in mind: run. But then he said something unpredictable. "Let me get my grams." He walked through the beaded doorway and disappeared into the back room.

His grams?

"Grams" wasn't at all what Addison expected when he came back into the room. Accompanying him was an old woman wearing a hippie-looking smock shirt. She had long, grey hair that was braided to one side and draped over her shoulder. She smiled, her beady eyes exuding the kind of excitement her mother possessed when she was alive. Addison's nerves subsided. "I'm Adele. What can I do for you, honey?" Grams said.

"I was told I could buy classic movies here, but I believe I was steered in the wrong direction. From the looks of it, you only sell new movies and electronics."

Among other things.

Adele sighed. "I had no choice. No one appreciates them anymore. Not when they can get them online for half the price."

"So your grandson works here?"

She nodded. "I know how he must look to you, but he's harmless. He runs this place now. A bit different than I did, of course. I pop in from time to time to say hello. You're lucky you caught me. Now what is it you're looking for?"

"Do you have any movies with Roxanne Rafferty?"

The woman breathed deeply and shook her head.

"Roxy Rafferty. Talented actress in her day. Poor girl. Police never found her. Did you know that?"

"You know about her movie career?"

The woman looked at Addison like she'd just asked if she knew gasoline was required to make a car drive. "First movie, *Stolen Kisses*, starring Miles Kent and Julie Devall. It was Roxy's first role. Next was *Lucky Star* with Wayne Cummings and Sally Sands. *Fly Me Away* was her first supporting role. That's where she met—"

"Hugh Brandon."

The woman beamed with pride. "You an old movie buff like me?"

"Just someone who's interested in Roxanne's work. But I guess you don't have any of those movies anymore," Addison said, glancing around.

"Come with me and we'll find out."

"You know a lot about movies. Is that from owning a store?"

"Partly. I was a stage hand once upon a time. Met a lot of actors that way: Audrey Hepburn and Rita Hayworth, or Rita Cansino as they once called her. It was my own little slice of heaven."

"Why did you quit?" Addison asked.

"I got married, had a baby. Decided to take some time off. I thought I could go back once my son started school. When I tried, they didn't need me anymore. They had more young kids lined up at the door for the job than they knew what to do with. So I packed it in and opened my own shop."

The woman walked through a doorway and pulled on a metal chain dangling from the ceiling. The light flickered a few times before beaming its rays throughout the vapid, time-worn room.

"What do you think?" the woman said, pointing to an old campaign book hanging on the wall beside her.

Addison inched forward, admiring the swirl pattern of the "C" and the "G," which looked more like the number nine than a letter. "Is that really Clark Gable's signature?"

"Watch the movie sometime. See if you recognize the girl walking the horse onto the track in the background."

"Was it you?"

Adele smiled. "Might be hard, of course; I wasn't even twenty years old when they filmed it." She walked over to a series of metal cabinets. "What movie did you say?"

"I'm really interested in the ones she did with Hugh Brandon and Phillip Edwards, but I'll take whatever you can find."

"Why those two—because they were her lovers?" she winked.

"It does make them seem a little more interesting."

"Sad story, what happened to Phillip Edwards. Fell from his horse while shooting an action scene in a western."

"He died?"

"Not from the fall, no. When Edwards hit the ground, the horse got spooked, kicking him in the head, repeatedly. They transported him to the hospital, but it didn't do much good. His skull had been fractured."

"What about the other guy?"

"Hugh Brandon?" she asked. "He made a few more movies after *Fly Me Away*. They sank faster than the Titanic. I haven't seen him in a movie since, actually."

"Do you know what happened to him?"

"Used to live around here. Maybe still does. Who knows? Most actors have homes all over the place." Adele stuck her hand into one of the file drawers and pulled out a VHS tape. "Here it is. *A Night in Paris*. Such a wonderful movie." She checked a few other drawers, carefully inspecting their contents. "I believe this is the only one I have that Miss Rafferty was in."

"What about Hugh's movies?"

"I might have *Keeper of Lies*...let me see." She fumbled around. "I'm sorry. I can't seem to find it. I hate to say this, but you might want to have a look online."

"I'm just glad you found one," Addison said, waving the tape around. "How much do I owe you?"

Adele swished a hand through the air. "Nothing. I haven't sold these for years. You have anything to watch it on?"

"All I have is a DVD player."

"Didn't imagine you'd have any use for a VCR. You can use one of mine."

"I'll return everything as soon as I'm finished."

"I've switched to a digital player myself. You can just toss it when you're done. I would like the video-tape back though, if it's not too much trouble. Memory's sake. Truth be told, *A Night in Paris* has always been one of my favorites. There's something magical about Roxy in that movie. You'll see. Even after all these years, you won't be able to take your eyes off of her. I just wish I could watch it without getting the thoughts out of my mind."

"What thoughts?"

Adele leaned back on a metal desk. "People like Roxy don't just disappear—not when they're on the brink of stardom like she was. You know, there was a lot of gossip going around just before she died. People said she had a secret lover no one knew about."

"How did they know?"

"Gossip is the same today as it ever was. There's always someone willing to roll over on a friend, especially when money's involved."

"Was the man ever identified?"

"It's been too long, honey. I don't remember."

"Have you ever heard the name Norman Grayson?"

"Hmm. Sounds vaguely familiar. But no. Can't place where I've heard it before." As Addison made her way to the door, Adele muttered, "Roxy liked to keep all her men on a string—play them against each other. Now, I'm not saying I'm right, but I'd be willing to bet that jealousy led to her undoing."

Finally, someone who believed the same thing she did. "You think she was murdered?"

Adele nodded. "And it sickens me that the son of a bitch got away with it."

CHAPTER 18

"Find what you were looking for?" Luke was just finishing up at the house when Addison walked in. Addison tossed the video tape into his lap. "*A Night In Paris*...it's a bit outdated, don't you think?"

"That's why we have this." She pulled the VCR out of a bag and held it out.

He took it and grinned. " *We?*"

She hesitated, second-guessing her choice of words. Luke flipped the boxed video cassette over, perusing the back side until something struck a chord. A name: Roxanne Rafferty. "This is the woman you texted me about. You found this at the library?"

"It was at an old video store. Well, at least it used to be a video store."

He raised a brow.

"It's a long story," she replied. "I bought pizza. It's in the car."

Luke stood. "I'll go get it."

"If you'd rather not stay, it's all right. I can just—"

He ran a hand over her arm as he passed by. "Oh, I'm staying."

The movie began several minutes later in typical Hollywood fashion with Roxanne Rafferty walking the cobbled streets of Paris—a woman down on her luck, broken and penniless, struggling to land a job, any job. Again and again she enters businesses seeking employment and is shooed away. Soaking wet and in a tattered dress, she tries one final office on the corner of a dead-end street. Her last hope. It's here she finds a man who takes pity on her, offering her a position he'd conveniently put in the paper a few short hours before. The pay isn't much, and it's not full time. But it's a job. She'll be his receptionist. She doesn't have the experience or the qualifications and has never typed a day in her life, but the man can't take his eyes off of her.

The woman at the video store had been right; Roxanne commanded an audience with vigor and ease. She didn't walk into a room, she waltzed into it. Head held high. Shoulders back, fluttering her big, brown eyes. Eyes filled with a dream.

"So that's her? Not bad," Luke said. "It must be strange for you to see her like this."

"She's different than I...imagined."

He clicked the pause button on the remote. "What is

it like—seeing someone who's dead?"

"You saw your grandfather; I could ask you the same thing."

"I never got a really good look at him. A bodiless head wasn't exactly something I could deal with at the time."

She leaned against the sofa cushion. "When my childhood friend fell from the swing, it seemed real—like I was there while it was happening, even though no one could hear me. The homeless man was almost like a bad dream I couldn't wake up from. I didn't understand why I was seeing him until they reported him dead on TV."

"What about Roxanne?"

"It's different with her. She can hear me. She knows I'm there. She hovered at the edge of the bed trying to tell me something. She has a purpose in being here. When I was in the room with her, I truly thought I could grab the gun out of the murderer's hands even though I couldn't. What's the point of knowing the outcome if there's no way to reverse it? She's dead. I can't bring her back."

Luke scooted closer. "Maybe that's not the point."

"Her murderer is probably dead by now."

"Then why is she here—why hasn't she moved on? What if she's stuck between this life and the next because her murder was never solved?"

An icy chill coursed through her body as she

considered his words. "Do you know how many unsettled spirits could be hanging around if that were true?"

She sat back and the movie resumed. The scene shifted. Roxanne sat on a wooden park bench alongside another working-class girl, legs crossed, both women anxious for the evening bus to arrive. Roxanne muttered a forced hello, as if obeying some predetermined societal rule and a timid conversation ensued. It was brief, and silence soon prevailed. All eyes were on the street, watching and willing the bus to come.

Addison sensed familiarity in the other woman's face. It was as if she'd seen her before. But that wasn't possible. How could it be? She stared at the screen, dissecting the woman's every move, searching for answers. The woman resembled Bette Davis; she had the same devilish grin and steely, mysterious eyes. It wasn't until the bus rounded the corner and both women rose from the bench that Addison found what she was looking for. The woman turned, bending down to grab her handbag. With a single flick of the wrist, the bag slid halfway up her arm. She reached over with her other hand and pulled it onto her shoulder.

It was a simple gesture and one no one would have noticed except a stunned Addison, who rose from the couch and inched closer, her eyes holding fast to the woman's every movement. She had seen the wrist flick before, but where? The answer surged through her in a wave of clarity as the woman ascended the steps, entered the bus, and handed something to the driver.

Helen.

The woman was a younger, more lively version of her aging neighbor. Addison turned away from the TV screen, her flesh prickling up and down her arms. She glanced at Luke. His body was curved, his eyes closed, mouth open—asleep. She wanted to wake him, but something stopped her. A finger, stiff and cold, traced down the side of her neck. It lasted only a second or two. And then it was gone. But Addison knew she was still there. The smell of rotting decay permeated the air, like fallen soldiers left on a battlefield.

Addison didn't move.

She didn't turn around.

She didn't face her.

"I know who you are," Addison whispered.

She waited.

"Can you hear me?"

She waited again. Had Roxanne gone?

An ethereal, shadowy vapor floated past Addison and turned before it reached the bottom of the stairs. Addison clamped her eyes shut and then opened them again, unable to believe the spectacle taking place. Hovering inches in front of her face was the ghost-like image of a bereaved, stern-faced Roxanne Rafferty.

Roxanne raised her arm into the air, prompting Addison to gaze upstairs.

"You want me to go up there?"

Roxanne tipped her head forward. The movement was slight, but her desires were clear. Addison climbed the stairs ahead of the waif-like figure, glancing back as she reached the top step. Roxanne was gone.

The door at top of the stairs opened to a glowing shower of iridescent light filtering layers of color through every door. Roxanne's body hung in the center of the hall, suspended in midair as if being held up by an invisible string. Her head was tilted back, her eyes closed. Her arms dangled from her sides, flaccid in appearance as if made of all flesh and no bone.

"Roxanne...can you hear me?"

Roxanne was unresponsive. Addison tiptoed forward, standing in front of Roxanne's lifeless body. Roxanne remained still in a trance-like state, her chest rising and falling. The doors to the one barricaded, locked room rattled loudly. Addison turned to look and held up a hand, shielding herself from the bright, blinding light surging from all the cracks and crevices of the door and its sidelites.

"Is that what you want?" Addison yelled. "You want me to go inside?" She backed away from the door and knelt down, suddenly gripped by a crushing feeling of fear, the kind of fear she felt the day her mother had died. The kind of fear she'd moved to get away from. She closed her eyes and buried her head inside her knees. "I can't," she whispered. "I don't want to go in there. I didn't want any of this. I know I'm supposed to help you, but I just want a normal life. I'm sorry…I'm so sorry."

When her eyes reopened, she was alone in the hallway. No blinding light. No rattling door. And no Roxanne.

CHAPTER 19

Addison didn't need to wake the locked room from its boarded-up state of slumber. She knew what she'd find on the other side. It was as if she'd always known. Ever since the night the knob had lit up like a glow-stick in front of her eyes, she'd been drawn to it. Maybe it was the reason she had resisted for so long. Even now, it was the one truth she didn't want to be real. With each passing day, she'd grown fonder of the manor. It was finally starting to feel like home. But how could she live in a place that harbored a deadly secret?

"There's something I haven't told you," Addison said, shaking Luke awake.

He half raised an eyelid, then closed it again. "Can we talk about it in the morning?"

"No—it has to be now," she insisted.

He sat up and rubbed his hands over his face. "What time is it?"

"I'm not sure."

"Did you finish the movie?" he asked.

"I was interrupted."

"By what?"

"By her."

"Roxanne?" he asked.

"She appeared to me."

"Here? In the living room?"

Addison nodded.

Luke shook his head. "And I slept right through it?"

"I had the feeling you wouldn't wake up even if I'd tried."

"What happened?" he asked.

"She wanted to show me something."

"What?"

"The bedroom upstairs."

"Which one?"

"The one that's locked."

Luke sat back, folded his arms and yawned. "So what have you been keeping from me?"

"Roxanne was murdered in that room, Luke."

"What? How can you possibly know that without ever seeing the room before?"

Addison sat down. "Trust me—I just do. I should have found a way to get into that room days ago."

"Why didn't you?"

Addison sighed. "I didn't want to deal with it. I don't

now. I want to help Roxanne, but I'm terrified, Luke. I don't care if I've been given some kind of curse where I can see dead—"

"It's a gift. Can't you see that? There are people out there who would give anything to see what you've seen."

"I don't care. I just want to live a normal life like everyone else."

He leaned across the couch, wrapping his fingers around her arms. "She chose you, Addison. Not me or the teenage kids who probably vandalized this place—you. You were chosen for a reason." He paused and then said, "I believe you are the only one who can set her free."

"I need more time. My mother just died. I haven't even recovered yet. I'm not ready for this. So I got curious, went to the library, got a video from an old woman and popped it in. Just because I can see her doesn't mean I can save her."

Luke tightened his grip. "That's what it is, isn't it? You want to help her, but you don't believe in yourself enough to know that you can."

She looked away. "I never said that."

"Is this how you want to spend your life, afraid of everything? Or are you going to start taking charge? You're not a little girl anymore, telling a story that no one believes. You know what you've seen is true. Don't you?"

She shrugged. "I guess so."

"You're a grown woman—you can do anything. You're stronger than you know, and you've got to start believing in yourself."

"Why?"

"Because I believe in you."

He believed in her. Never in her life had anyone said those words. Roxanne was restless. Addison had seen the frustration in her pallid eyes. She couldn't let her down.

Luke stood and smiled, staring at Addison like he'd finally seen the spark that he'd been waiting for.

"Where are you going?" she asked.

"To break that door down."

CHAPTER 20

Addison expected Luke to reappear with an axe in hand. He didn't.

"You're going to break the door down…with that?" she asked.

He smiled. "Watch and learn, grasshopper." He pointed at the corner of the door. "See these hinges? They're on the outside. Most of the time, they're on the inside. I should just be able to tap the hinge pins out, and then I can pull the door off."

"You just pull it off?"

"Remove it from the frame? Yeah."

Luke and his hammer went to work on the first pin. Fifteen minutes later, it hadn't budged.

"This door has been here for so long, these pins have practically become fused to it," he said. "If I oiled them, it might help, but it might not either. I might have to break it down after all."

"Isn't there a way to get these doorknobs off?"

"It's locked from the inside, and the outside is solid. There's no hole."

"How did they get in here if it was locked from the outside?"

"Maybe that was the idea. Once they locked it, they never planned on going inside again."

"What now?" she asked.

He laughed. "Roxanne, if you can hear me, we could use some help."

"Luke, I don't think you should say things like…"

A cracking noise was heard on the other side of the door, followed by what sounded like pieces of something shattering.

"Did you hear that?" Luke asked. "Sounded like broken glass."

"It came from behind this," Addison said, placing her hands on top of one of the long wood boards. "We need to get one of these off."

Luke replaced the hammer with a pry bar, splitting the wood until he'd broken off a chunk large enough for Addison to stick a hand through. She turned the middle of the knob until it clicked and stared into the murky darkness.

"You want to turn the light on?" she asked Luke.

"Nope. This is all you."

Addison ran her hand along the inside of the wall

until she felt the switch. She turned it. The light sputtered on.

"It's empty," she said. "There's nothing here."

"What did you expect to find?"

"I don't know. Not this."

"Look again—what do you see?"

There were holes in the walls but no pictures. A half-open closet door with a few wire hangers but no clothing. There was one window. The carpeting on the floor was thin and brown and reminded her of something she'd see at church. "Strange."

"What?"

"The carpet. All of the rooms in the house are hardwood. None of them have carpet. Not even the storage closet."

"Exactly."

Addison walked around the room, staring at the walls, trying to remember where she'd seen Roxanne crouched in the corner, begging for her life. On the wall opposite the door she found a tiny hole. It was too small to be a bullet hole or a nail, but the perfect size for a pushpin. "This is where the calendar was—which means Roxanne was right about here when I saw her in my vision. I remember the floor. There was no carpet. It was wood."

Luke reached into his pocket and retrieved a carpenter's knife. "With your permission?"

Addison nodded. "Rip it out. Rip it *all* out."

CHAPTER 21

Beneath the carpet was a spot. A really big spot. A really old spot. But it wasn't blood. It was a splintered, circular pattern extending six feet in all directions. The rich mahogany color of the wood was faded to a much lighter shade that looked like it had been scrubbed several times over. Addison bent to her knees, feeling the roughness of the wood with her hand.

"Someone cleaned this," Luke said, kneeling beside her.

"And once the police came around looking for Roxanne, they knew they had to do something, so they slapped a piece of carpeting over it."

"It's still here, so it must have worked."

"So, what do we do now—call the police?"

"Do you think they'll believe you?" Luke asked. "All we have is a faded patch of wood, and an old, stained dress, which may or may not be stained with blood, possibly pointing to a female killer. And we don't have a body."

"Yet," Addison said.

Possible blood and no body. What *had* been done with Roxanne's body? A chilling sense of clarity swept over Addison as she realized an undeniable truth: Roxanne couldn't have been killed in her grandparents' house without them knowing about it. Were they to blame? Had the dress belonged to her grandmother? And if so, had she taken the responsibility of Roxanne's death to her grave? Addison thought about how adamant her mother had been about shunning her grandmother for all those years. Had she been there that night—had she seen something? She glanced back at the floor. It didn't matter how many times it had been bleached, the overwhelming smell of death lingered like an abandoned city morgue.

"I will go to the police," Addison said, "and hopefully someone who was working the case all those years ago is alive today. If I can get anyone to believe me, it would be one of the detectives who investigated her disappearance in the first place. But there's something I need to do before that."

Addison and Luke returned to the living room. She rewound the video-tape and pressed play.

"What are we looking for?" Luke asked.

"See that woman on the bench?" Addison pointed. "I

am almost positive she's my neighbor."

"The old woman who brought you the pie? She's so young. How can you tell?"

"It's her mannerisms. She moves just like she did back then."

Luke looked closer at the screen. "I don't see anything unusual."

"I know it's her," Addison stated. She fast-forwarded the tape until the end credits rolled and read the names of the cast members aloud. In the "also starring" category was Roxanne Rafferty. It took another minute or two for Addison to find what she was looking for, an actress known as the "lady on the bench." Only her name wasn't Helen. It was Vivian Bouvier.

"Did she introduce herself when you two met?" Luke asked.

"She said her name was Helen. She never gave her last name."

"Then it's not her."

"Vivian could be her stage name."

"It's nearly five in the morning—you'll have to wait a few hours, maybe more, before you can find out." Luke said.

Addison yawned. "I'm going to try to get some sleep."

"I can stay on the couch if you want, in case anything happens."

"I'll be fine. Thank you for staying with me

through…well…everything. I know I was a mess earlier, but everything has changed now."

And it had. She didn't know why or how, only that she felt like a new woman was emerging inside of her—a woman who wasn't scared or afraid of the unknown. In fact, she was fearless.

CHAPTER 22

Helen didn't look the least bit astonished to see Addison standing on her doorstep. But then, Addison assumed not much shocked the woman at her age.

"I wondered when you'd stop by and see me," Helen said, ushering Addison in. "How is the house coming along, dear?"

"Just fine."

Addison glanced around the room. A faint whiff of perfume permeated the air. It smelled familiar, like a fragrance created by Coco Chanel. A grand piano rested peacefully in the corner, giving the impression that it was used more often as a place to rest one's wine glass than a spot people gathered for a festive sing-along. On the far wall was an array of black-and-white photos grouped together in three rows. There were at least thirty head shots, and all of them had been signed by the actor or actress in the picture. Most were of people she wasn't familiar with, but there were a few familiar faces in the mix: Greer Garson, Lana Turner, and even a smug-faced Marlon Brando looking hunky and svelte, a far cry from the man he became in later days.

"Where did you get all of these pictures?" Addison asked.

Helen's eyes sparkled with delight. "Oh, here and there over the years." She took her cane and angled it at one of the photographs Addison didn't recognize. "Bob's my favorite."

Addison stepped closer. "I don't know him."

"Don't you?" She shook her head. "I suppose you wouldn't. Shame, really. Mitchum was one of the greats of his day. Now then, why don't we sit, and you can tell me why you've come."

Addison did as requested, taking a seat across from Helen, who stared back at her like she was some kind of bubble-gum-toting kid she'd never fully understand and didn't want to, even if she could.

Addison took a moment to rehearse the words she'd mulled over at least a dozen times. "I was thinking about the day we first met," she began. "You never answered my question."

"Which question was that?"

"Why did my grandmother leave the manor?"

The old woman's shoulders bobbed up and down as if on cue. "What makes you think I know?"

"You were friends, weren't you?" Addison asked. "That's what you said."

"We weren't attached at the hip, if that's what you're suggesting. She didn't tell me everything. Why does it matter now anyway? You said she was dead. Let her rest in peace."

Addison brushed off her smug reply and persisted. "You're evading the question, even now. Do you know what made my grandmother leave, or don't you?"

Helen's face hardened. "No. I do not. One day she was here, the next she was gone. Satisfied?"

Far from it. As her mouth opened to ask her next question, a shrill, clattering sound rang out from a back room, the sound mimicking pieces of tin hitting the floor.

"What was that?" Addison asked.

Helen's eyes widened, and she flicked her wrist, just like she'd done in the movie. "What was what? I don't hear anything."

"The noise I just heard. There's no way you didn't hear it."

Addison stood.

"What are you doing? Sit down!" Helen shrieked.

Helen's words fell on a deaf and determined Addison, who buzzed down the hall like a bee's stinger set to maximum impact. "Hello? Who's back there?"

Silence.

"Hello? Come out. I know you can hear me."

Addison neared the door, flattened her hand, and pushed the door open. A miniature tan-and-white ball of fur with a haircut resembling a baby lioness bounded down the hall and into the living room, where it sought reprieve in the arms of its owner. A slender, wrinkly-faced man limped not far behind.

"I thought you said you lived alone," Addison said, whipping around.

"I do," Helen replied. "He's my help."

"Your *help?*"

What century is this woman living in?

"I'm sorry, ma'am," the man said. "She got away from me."

"That's all right, Milton. Take her for a walk, would you?"

The dog spun around a few times, then curled into a ball on Helen's lap.

Helen rolled her eyes. "Oh, never mind. Give us a minute, won't you?"

Milton nodded and shuffled out of the room.

Helen eyed Addison curiously. "Well, are you going to sit back down now, or is there something else you want to check out first?"

The more time Addison spent with Helen, the more she despised that authoritative tone in her crackly voice. All her life she'd listened to others, doing what they wanted her to do—taking advice instead of following her own intuition. But not today. Today the bone in her back felt straighter. She held her head higher. She meant what she'd said to Luke the night before; she *did* feel different. A change was taking place inside her, and although she didn't know where it would lead, she knew she'd never be the same again.

"Milton has been with me for over fifty years," Helen remarked.

"I'm not here to talk about him. I want to talk about you, Vivian. That *is* your name, isn't it?"

The old woman stroked the dog, her rumpled, spotted hands beginning to tremble. "No one has called me that in a long time. How did you know?"

"I saw a movie last night. *A Night in Paris*."

"How did you recognize me?"

"You still move the same."

"I don't understand," Helen said.

"Your hand gestures. They haven't changed."

Helen gave a slight nod. "No one has noticed me in years. Not that I get out much anymore. I'd rather stay here where it's quiet. I've been out of the limelight for several decades now. If you knew anything about the business, you'd understand why I chose the simple life in the end."

Addison crossed one leg over the other. "So which is it—Helen or Vivian?"

"Helen Bouvier. My father was French." She glanced

out the window. "I've never been to France myself. I was raised here in America. In any case, the studio execs loved Bouvier, but they weren't so keen on Helen. They said Helen sounded like the name of a bored housewife. Vivian, on the other hand, had a touch of flair. So that's who I became."

"Were you in a lot of movies?"

"Several. Never aspired to my goal as lead actress though. I never even starred as a supporting actress. Your grandfather got me a role in *Ride the West Wind* that turned out to be the best speaking part I ever had. I thought there would be more, until he left town."

Addison's jaw tightened. "My grandfather? What did he have to do with acting?"

Helen shook her head. "It surprises me that your mother never told you any of this. Your grandfather, Norman Grayson, was an assistant director in Hollywood. He was a very important man in his day."

"If that's true, why would he give it all up like he did?"

"You can't imagine the stress he was under. The kind of stress that ages a person far beyond their years. He was tired of the game—he wanted out and he got out."

The revelations kept coming. *What else don't I know?*

"You must have known my grandfather well then if he got you parts in his movies."

She shrugged. "Well enough. There was a group of us who had apartments in and around Hollywood but preferred life elsewhere when we weren't on set."

"So the manor wasn't my grandparents' only residence?"

"Oh no, dear. They rented a lovely home in Hollywood. I always thought your grandmother would end up there, but she sold the place, something I'll never understand."

Helen gave the dog a gentle nudge, and he hopped to the floor. She grabbed the cane next to her and scooted to the edge of the chair. "If you'll excuse me, Addison, I have to take a ride to the city in a few minutes. Thank you for coming to visit. I don't get much company these days. I'll give you my phone number in case you find yourself in need of anything else."

"There's something I need right now."

Helen raised a brow. "Oh, what's that?"

"I want you to tell me what you know about Roxanne Rafferty."

CHAPTER 23

If uttering Roxanne Rafferty's name out loud came as a surprise to Helen, she didn't show it. Her composure remained the same, her tired eyes not registering any sudden movement that would give away her innermost thoughts. She twisted her cane back and forth with the palm of her hand and stared straight ahead, choosing her next words carefully. "Why are you asking about Roxy—is it because of the movie? No one knows where she—"

"I know all of that already."

"What exactly do you think you know?" Helen snapped.

"Roxanne went missing after attending a party at the manor. She was never seen again."

"Is that why you're so curious—because of the scandalous history behind her disappearance? You're wasting your time. That was ages ago."

"I'm interested in a lot of things."

"Such as?"

"How you knew her."

"From the movie set, of course. There's no reason to hide it, so I won't."

"Did she attend many of my grandparents' parties?"

"I don't remember seeing Roxanne at more than one or two. She wasn't a staple like some of the others."

"What about the night she went missing—did you see her then?"

Helen shook her head. "I had an audition in California."

"For what?"

"A role I never got."

"What was the name of the movie?"

"Why do I get the feeling I'm being interrogated?"

"I'm just asking a few simple questions."

Helen squirmed in her seat. "I get the feeling it's a lot more than that. You're meddling into something you shouldn't.

"I read in the newspaper that my grandfather went missing that same night. Were they having an affair?"

"Norman and Roxy—how would I know?"

"You were their neighbor," Addison stated. "I'm sure you heard things."

"I wasn't here that night. I already told you."

"Did you know Roxanne well?"

"Not really. We talked a few times on set or when we saw one another at social gatherings."

"Who else was at that party the night she went missing?"

"I don't know. I never asked. Now—as I said before, I have an appointment to get to." Helen stood and called for the help. He came quickly, as though he'd been standing in the next room, listening and waiting.

Addison sighed, her hope of learning something useful from Helen drifting away like an inflatable raft tossed around an unruly ocean. She was about to leave—disappointed at having gotten only meager explanations to her queries when one last question entered her mind. She pivoted on her heel. "Do you remember the names of the detectives who worked on the case?"

"How could I forget? They hounded me and everyone else I knew that first year."

"Why?"

"The public demanded answers, and they thought if they kept interviewing us, eventually someone would change their story."

"I'd like the names of the detectives."

"Dobbs and Houston. Why do you want them so badly? What's your motivation in all of this?"

Addison's stomach lurched. She crossed her arms in front of her and looked Helen in the eye, amazed at how hard it was to speak the simple truth. "I…I believe

Roxanne was murdered."

Helen's gasp resonated throughout every corner of the valley. She smacked her cane down on the tile floor with both hands and stood firmly behind it. "Now wait just a minute! Why would you say something like that?"

"I'm not the only one to suspect foul play."

"But there isn't any proof."

"I'm entitled to my own opinion. I don't need any proof for that."

Helen fell silent and remained that way for over several seconds. "I shouldn't be telling you this, but I don't see what harm it will do now. There was a rumor going around the time of Roxanne's disappearance."

Addison stifled a smile—finally she was getting somewhere. "What was it?"

"Supposedly your grandfather and Roxanne were having an affair. For how long, I never knew. Someone found out about it and told the producer of the movie he was working on."

"But you just said you didn't know if they were having an affair," Addison said.

"I also said I needed to leave, and since you're standing in my way, I've decided that since you want the truth so badly, why not give it to you? You seem to think you can take it."

"Go on."

"If the affair turned out to be true, and I never knew

if it was, it would have been a big deal at the time because the producer accused your grandfather of convincing the studio he worked for to hire Roxanne for roles in movies that should have gone to other actresses. Something like that could have ruined his career."

"And you believe that's why he left?"

"I believe it's why they *both* left. In my opinion, she went first and he followed once a little time had passed. You asked me if I knew why your grandmother left the manor. I don't. But I imagine living there after finding out everyone in Hollywood suspected her husband of messing around behind her back would have been enough to break any woman."

CHAPTER 24

It couldn't be true. Addison had seen Roxanne. She'd seen the room, held the stained dress in her hand. Helen's confession was spoken like she was under oath, testifying with one rigid hand flattened over the Bible. She believed Norman and Roxanne had run off together, and had most likely given this theory to Detectives Dobbs and Houston.

A call to the local police department yielded nothing. The sprightly, young secretary who answered explained she didn't have time to look up anything about the case "right now." She took Addison's name and number and said she'd have someone call her back "at their earliest convenience."

Addison needed a distraction while she passed the time, and she found it in Hugh Brandon, one of Roxanne Rafferty's supposed lovers. There were three Hugh Brandons listed in the phone book. Addison considered calling first, then decided showing up in person was best. No one could hang up on her that way, and if a door was slammed in her face, she'd just wait around until it reopened again.

The first Hugh Brandon turned out to be a thirty-something investment banker who didn't spend much time at home, a testament his neighbor was all too happy to give.

Two more to go.

Adjacent to Central Park was one of the most architecturally sublime condominium communities Addison had ever seen. The Pallisades was a pre-1900, highly sought-after residence most people couldn't afford if they lived a dozen lifetimes. It came complete with a gloved bellman at the door and a mirrored elevator that looked like it had been dipped in gold. Addison stepped inside and pressed the button for the third floor. She found the right apartment number and knocked. No one came. She knocked again, this time hearing a faint, "Hang on," wafting through a tiny crack.

A stunning, leggy, young girl opened the door. She had long, blond hair-extensions, Addison surmised, that ran halfway down her back and the waifish figure of a person who nibbled nothing more than a few bites of rabbit food each day.

"I must have the wrong address. Sorry to bother you." Addison shook her head, disappointed. She'd struck out—again. Or had she?

The girl scanned over Addison's less-than-model-worthy body, repeatedly flicking the metal zipper pull on her fur vest with the tip of her fingernail. The cropped vest exposed her pierced belly button and appeared to have nothing beneath it. "Are you looking for someone?"

"Hugh Brandon. He was an—"

"Actor."

Addison rested a hand on her hip. "You know who he is?"

"He's my dad, I'd better."

Impossible.

"You look a little young to be his daughter."

She rolled her eyes indicating she'd heard that particular line many times before. "I was adopted. Long story." She glanced at the screen of her pink bedazzled cell phone. "Anyway, my dad's not here right now, so…"

"Is there some place I can wait?"

A woman appeared behind the girl. She looked old enough to be Hugh Brandon's wife. She had pale, greyish-blue eyes and wore a button up rayon blouse and black trousers. Never before had Addison seen a woman so fit for her age. "Who's this?" The woman gestured toward Addison.

The girl wiggled her arms up and down. "She never said her name, Mom."

"Addison Lockhart."

"I'm Celeste," the woman said. "Celeste Brandon." The younger girl smiled and disappeared back inside the house. "How can we help you, Addison?"

"I don't think you can. I'm looking for Hugh."

"What do you want with him?"

Addison was unsure of what to say next. "I just moved here. Well, not here. I inherited a house in Rhinebeck from my mother."

Celeste tipped her head forward, her interest piqued. "I know several people who live in Rhinebeck. Which house, dear?"

"Grayson Manor."

Several seconds passed before the woman spoke again. "You said *inherited.* Do you mean to say you're related to Norman and Marjorie Grayson in some way?"

"I'm their granddaughter."

The woman swung the door all the way open. "You'd better come inside."

CHAPTER 25

The interior of Celeste Brandon's home looked like it had been ripped from the pages of *Architectural Digest* magazine. It was white, from the crisp, clean walls to the furniture. Massive, colorful artwork was depicted on almost every wall, one or two even larger than the picturesque windows overlooking the park.

Celeste craned her neck. "Follow me to the study, please."

Addison kept pace behind her.

"Are you expecting your husband anytime soon?"

"He's flying back in tonight. Now—I want to show you something." She opened the top drawer of a desk and retrieved one item: an album. She licked a finger and flipped through page after page, stopping when she got to the middle. "Ah, here it is." She turned the album around and curled her finger, motioning Addison to step forward. "This is your grandfather, but I suppose you can tell just by looking at it."

"Actually, I haven't seen many photos of him until recently."

Very recently.

"I was told he ran off, leaving my grandmother to take care of my mother on her own."

Celeste snapped the book shut and held it to her chest, her arms folded over it. "Yes, he did. Although I never saw it coming. I was as shocked as everyone else when I heard the news."

"Why?"

"Because I could tell he loved her."

"My grandmother?"

"Yes," Celeste replied. "They seemed to get on so well together every time I was around. Though, your grandfather…"

Celeste tapped a finger over her lips as if she wished she could take back her last few words.

"What is it?"

"Nothing, dear. Best to leave the past where it is."

"You can tell me. Really. I don't mind."

"It's just that your grandfather, kind as he was, had a wandering eye from time to time. I'm not speculating. I wouldn't have said it if I wasn't absolutely sure."

"How do you know?"

"He admitted it once."

"To you?"

"To Hugh."

"Did my grandmother know?"

Celeste nodded. "She stayed, in spite of it. He promised never to do it again. But then he would. He was kind of like a revolving door, if you ask me."

"Who were the women—did you know any of them?"

"Hugh never told me, and I didn't ask."

Addison found Celeste's statement very odd. It was a rare woman who had no interest in idle gossip. "How well did you know them?"

"We met at Grayson Manor. Your grandparents loved throwing parties. And I loved attending them. Hugh was always away making one movie or another and most of the time I was alone. Your grandmother did her best to make me feel like I was a part of the business, even though I wasn't. But then again, neither was she. Not really."

Addison nervously gnawed on the side of her lip.

"Do you want to ask me something?" Celeste asked. "Because you can, you know. You still haven't told me why you're here."

"I don't want to be inconsiderate."

"Of what—my feelings?" Celeste curled a hand over her mouth, suppressing a laugh. "I doubt there's anything you could shock me with at my age."

"I'm not sure."

"Try me. I'm a lot tougher than this feeble, shell of a body appears to be."

Addison cleared her throat and tried to control her breathing. "I came here today to ask Hugh about his rumored romance with Roxanne Rafferty." She stepped back, waiting for the aftershocks from the bomb she'd just exploded all over the room.

None came.

Celeste simply nodded.

"Roxy was one of many girls my husband *supposedly* slept with. He was a big flirt, my Hugh. Got him into trouble several times. But you know something? I've never given much stock to rumors—especially Hollywood ones. You know what they say…if it makes it to the paper, odds are, it isn't true."

"Did you ever ask him?"

"Hugh denied he had affairs with all of the women he acted with, and I believed him. Maybe that was naïve of me, I don't know. Nothing was ever proven, and he's always treated me like I'm the only thing that matters to him in life. Truth is, I was too smitten with him to ever leave, even if I'd found out he had cheated."

"Roxanne was friendly with several other men too."

"Contrary to what you may have read, Roxy was one of the nicest girls I've ever met. Men fell all over her, and yes, some of them were married. But I never got the impression that she went after them. They beat down her door and there wasn't much she could do about it. I suppose she was flattered, just like any woman would be."

Celeste's unflappable nature inspired Addison to press on. "Did anyone ever talk to you about the night Roxanne went missing?"

"There were whispers, theories. Some wild, others ridiculous. Leave women alone in a room together for too long, regardless of their age, wild stories are sure to follow. We can't help ourselves, I suppose."

"There were suspicions of foul play."

"Isn't there always? Tabloids will say anything to sell a story." Celeste opened the drawer, placed the photo album back inside and slid the drawer shut again. "Now I have a question for you. Why are you worrying your head over all of this?"

Addison plucked a white lie from her mental file cabinet. "I saw some pictures of Roxanne in an old trunk I found. Then someone told me she was dead. And that the last time she was seen was at my grandparents' house, which is now my house. It made me curious."

"You came all this way to ask a question because you're *curious?*"

"I guess I just can't stop thinking about what happened to her. I've been experiencing some…ahh…nightmares."

"You'll forgive me if I have to sit down," Celeste said,

pulling a chair out. She looked as if she was about to faint. "You're welcome to have a seat yourself."

"Thank you, I'm fine."

"Are you?"

"I don't understand."

Celeste entwined her fingers, resting them on the edge of the desk. "What is it you *really* want to ask?"

"What do you think happened to her, Mrs. Brandon?"

Celeste twisted a gold ring in circles around her finger. "You understand if I tell you, it's only my opinion, right? It doesn't make it fact."

Addison nodded and waited, her heart beating wildly inside her chest.

"I mentioned that I had spoken to Roxy right before she died about a role she was auditioning for. During the conversation, she said she was going up against another actress who'd left her threatening phone calls."

"What kind of threatening phone calls—what was said?"

"Apparently, the other actress said she'd been promised the role until Roxy's name had been thrown into the mix."

"Let me guess—my grandfather suggested the director audition Roxanne?"

"He did. This angered the other actress enough for her to make some pretty outrageous phone calls."

"What was the name of the actress?"

"Dottie Davis."

Addison thanked Celeste for her time and left with one goal in mind: she needed to find her grandfather.

CHAPTER 26

Pale shades of coral splashed with a touch of blue dotted the horizon like ribbons in the wind, following the sun as it made its grand departure. It was Addison's favorite time of day. She could sit and stare at the vivid array of colors for hours. But not tonight. Something else grabbed her attention. When she turned down the road for home, a man sat on her front porch, his legs crossed, arms folded. He looked much too old to be Luke; even from a distance Addison could see that. As she drove closer, she could see his broad, greyish-colored beard and the funny-looking hat on top of his head. It was brown and in the style of something Frank Sinatra used to wear on his album covers.

She exited the car and he stood, offering his hand to her when she drew near. "It's Miss Lockhart, right?"

They shook hands.

"Can I help you?" she asked.

"Name's Houston."

He said it like it should mean something to her. It didn't. She offered a cautious smile. "Why are you here?"

"Heard you were looking for me."

"From…?"

"I'm sorry," he said. "From what I was told, I thought you were expecting me."

A light inside Addison's head sparked on. *Detective* Houston. "I'm glad you're here."

They went inside. Addison offered him a glass of water, which he accepted, hastily drinking it down in a few swallows like he'd been parched for days.

"I have some questions about a case you worked on many years ago," Addison said.

He nodded. "Since I'm here, I'll take a stab at it and say it's the Rafferty case. What's got you so interested?"

"I'm sure you'll remember this house was the last place she was seen."

He stammered a barely audible, "I do."

"Can you tell me who else was here the night she disappeared?" Addison asked. "I assume you interviewed everyone."

He fiddled with his beard. "I did. Can't remember all the names, though. Not off the top of my head."

"Don't you have any records or paperwork from that night?"

He placed a hand on the arm of the sofa. "Mind if I

sit?" After he sat down, he continued. "I'm retired. And I'll be honest, I've thought of Miss Rafferty many times over the years. It was good to step away from it all, clear my mind. My life is simple now. I want to keep it that way."

Any hope Addison had of the detective helping her turned to disappointment. He was old, he was tired, and he didn't seem to care. "It doesn't bother you that the case was never solved?"

"Never said that. I just don't think of it much anymore. Can't solve them all."

His lack of compassion startled her, making her wonder if too many years in that line of work changed a person. "Your files—the ones you would have kept with the names of those you'd interviewed that night. They'd be at the station, right?"

He shrugged. "S'pose so."

"I can give them a call. Then you don't need to concern yourself with it."

He shook his head. "That won't be necessary. I'll get them. But first, I'd like to know what all of this is about."

Addison sat across from him, her mind filled with a handful of scenarios, which she weighed one by one. He was a detective. He'd know if she was hiding something. A direct approach was needed. "Do you think it's possible that Roxanne was murdered?" Addison looked him square in the eyes, gauging his reaction.

He shifted on his seat, a startled look covering his face that he tried to hide. It was pointless; she'd seen it already. "Miss Lockhart, I need to know who you are and why you're asking these questions if you want this conversation to continue any further."

"All right," she replied, tucking her feet beneath her legs. "I inherited Grayson Manor recently."

"From?"

"My mother."

"You'll forgive me if I don't follow. I have no idea what became of this place once my investigation was over. Who was your mother?"

"Maybe this will help. I'm the granddaughter of Norman and Marjorie Grayson."

He jerked his head back. The connection had been made. "It still doesn't explain to me why the sudden interest in Miss Rafferty."

"I have reason to believe Roxanne Rafferty was murdered."

The man sat, silently digesting her words. He didn't move. He didn't speak. He just stared at her, the discomfort spreading throughout the room like a thick blanket. Not knowing what else to do, she kept going. "I know it sounds crazy, but I—"

He held a hand out as if to shush her. "I see."

He sees? He sees what exactly?

He tugged on his beard. This time, she kept quiet. If

he had something to say, she'd wait to hear it. One minute passed. Then two. He looked at her. She looked back, refusing to break the silence. Another minute went by before it paid off.

"There hasn't been any new information for years. And here you are broadcasting your opinion like you were there. Forgive me, but you weren't. You know nothing about it."

His arrogance clung to the air like a hefty puff of cigar smoke. "Do you think someone killed her or don't you?"

"Maybe. Possibly. Hell, I don't know. I had several suspicions back then, none I could prove."

"Did you have any suspects?"

"There were a few people we looked at more than others."

"Who?"

"I'd rather not say."

"Even after all this time? Why does it matter now? I believe she may have been murdered—here in this house."

He shook his head. "Impossible. My partner and I searched every room. We didn't find anything to prove Miss Rafferty was harmed here."

"Then you didn't look hard enough."

"What are you saying?"

"I need to show you something." She stood. "I found

evidence in one of the rooms in this house. Two rooms, actually."

"What do you mean *two rooms?*"

"One I believe she was murdered in, the other contained a dress that appears to have dried blood on it. I'd like to know how it can be tested to see if I'm right."

He looked at her like she'd lost her mind, but followed her up the stairs anyway. "It's in here." Addison pushed the door open, flicked the light switch, and stepped back, allowing him to view the discoloration of the wood on the opposite side of the room.

"Their daughter's room?"

Addison gasped. It couldn't be true. Her mother's room? "What do you mean?"

"This was their daughter's room. Nothing could have happened here. The child was asleep in this room on the night of the party."

A sudden uneasiness spread through Addison's body. Her legs twitched, buckling beneath her. She reached out a hand, grappling for the wall next to her.

"Are you all right?" he asked.

"I…I don't think so. The stain on the floor there. I thought someone had cleaned something up, and then covered it with carpet when the wood faded."

"This carpeting was here the first time I questioned Mr. and Mrs. Grayson, and it didn't appear to be new at the time. I would have noticed."

"I don't understand. Why was the room boarded up?"

"Boarded up?"

Addison pointed to the strips of wood, some still covering the door. "When I arrived, the door to this room was locked. I couldn't get in. Boards had been nailed over the glass. Whoever went to the trouble didn't want anyone in here—ever."

He reached behind her, picking up one of the boards. He inspected both sides, then let it fall to the floor again. "I can't say. It wasn't boarded up when I was here. There have been vandals over the years. Maybe that's why this room was locked up."

"But there wasn't anything in it," Addison said. "Why this room and none of the others? Who would take the time to lock it up? My grandfather hasn't been seen since the murder, and my grandmother is dead."

The man shuddered. "What do you mean, *dead?*"

"You didn't know?"

"I haven't spoken to her since my investigation. How?"

Addison shook her head. "I don't know. I wasn't a part of her life."

"What—why?"

"I'd rather not go into it."

He offered a look of understanding. "Did you say there was something else—a dress?"

Addison walked across the hall toward her room, the weight of her feet felt like giant bags filled with sand. Would he find fault with the dress too? Everything was unraveling. It didn't make sense. None of it did. She removed the dress box from beneath her bed and lifted the lid, extending it out to him.

"Aren't you going to take it out?" he asked.

She couldn't. Not without touching it. "You can," she said, placing the box into his hands.

He reached a hand inside the box and lifted the dress. It unraveled, revealing the stained blemishes across the front. "You believe these spots are blood?"

Addison nodded. "I'm not the expert, but it looks like blood to me."

He reached into the briefcase-like bag he'd been carrying, pulled out a pair of glasses, and put them on. "Hard to tell. It could be anything. Where did you find this?"

"In an old chest in one of the storage rooms."

The man inspected both sides of the dress, pressing his face as close as he could without touching it. "I don't think this is blood."

"What then?"

"Wine, maybe. Hard to say for sure."

"Can it be tested?" Addison asked.

"Let me talk to a few people and see what I can do. Would you like me to take the dress with me now?"

She considered it. If she dared touch the dress again, it *had* to remain with her. She had more questions now than ever.

"I'd like to keep it. If they are willing to test it for blood, I'll take it in myself."

He slanted his head toward the side and lifted his brow like he couldn't understand her attachment to a piece of clothing that didn't even belong to her. "Well, here you go then," he said, holding it out.

Addison jerked back.

"What's the matter?" he asked.

"My...umm...hands are dirty. I don't want to get anything else on it. Could you put it back for me?" It wasn't the perfect response, but it was the only thing she could think of to say.

He eyed her suspiciously and then did what she asked. When the lid was closed, she took it from him, sliding it back underneath the bed.

"Knock, knock," Luke yelled from downstairs. "Addison, you here?"

"Excuse me a minute," she said.

"A friend?" the man asked.

"He's..." Luke *had* become a friend, someone she trusted. The thought of their growing relationship caused her to smile without even being aware of it.

The man cleared his throat. "You were saying?"

"He's restoring the house for me."

She walked to the top of the stairs and called down. "Luke, there's someone I want you to meet."

Introductions were made, followed by the former detective saying he had to be going. Addison and Luke followed him outside where he promised to be in touch again over the next couple of days.

After he'd gone, Luke turned. "Is he the actual person who worked the case? How did you find him so fast?"

But Addison wasn't listening. She narrowed her eyes, staring at the house.

"What is it?" Luke asked.

Something wasn't right.

CHAPTER 27

Cabinets slammed. Drawers opened, then banged shut again. An angry, hurricane-like wind tore through the air, ripping the living room curtains from their rods and tossing them from wall to wall like rag dolls. Luke's mouth gaped open. He stepped inside, shielding his eyes with a hand as if trudging through a sandstorm.

"She's angry," Addison yelled. Her hair swirled around, slapping against her face.

"Why—what happened?"

"I don't know."

"You have to. Think. What did you talk about with the detective—did he say anything to cause it?"

The chaos around her made it difficult to concentrate. She ran through the conversation in her mind, the detective's words resounding in her head. He'd shot down just about every assumption she'd made, all the while remaining in a neutral state. He didn't disagree, he didn't agree either. And Roxanne had been there to hear it all. Maybe that's what had her so upset. If Detective Houston cared what happened to her once upon a time, he didn't anymore.

"I got the impression he didn't believe me," Addison said. "He had sound objections for everything I presented. In the bedroom, he said the carpet had always been there, which meant the stain was from something predating the murder. It can't be true—it just can't."

"What about the dress?"

"He didn't say it *wasn't* blood. He suggested it might be nothing more than spilled wine."

"Why doesn't he just have it tested?"

"He offered to take it," Addison said. "I didn't want to give it to him."

"Why not? You need answers. How else are you going to get them?"

"You know why. I need to return to that night one more time. I feel like I've missed something. I was sure Roxanne died in that room. I need to see it again."

A knife flew through the air, narrowly missing Luke's face. Other silverware followed, all directed toward the door. It was as if Roxanne was playing a game of darts, using the door as her dartboard.

"You have to do something!" Luke yelled.

"Like what?"

"I don't know—see if you can get through to her."

"She's not alive. It's not like I can control a spirit."

Luke wrapped a hand around Addison's wrist. "This has to stop! She's tearing the house apart."

"You should go."

He shook his head. "No way. I'm not leaving."

"She won't hurt me, Luke. Please."

He didn't budge.

Addison breathed in. The words stuck in her throat like a thick, rubbery mass had lodged there, making it almost impossible to speak. "Roxanne, stop," she croaked.

Roxanne was not swayed by her soft words.

"It's not working," Addison moaned.

Luke placed a hand on her shoulder. "Try again. Let her know you mean it."

"What if—"

"Try again, Addison."

She stretched her hands all the way out in front of her, fingers spread. She *would* get through this time. She had to. "Roxanne! This is *my* house. You *will* stop this. Now."

The silverware clanked to the ground, the drapes fluttering into a sagging heap over them. Once again, the house was silent.

"Nice job," Luke said, patting her on the back.

But something was wrong. She couldn't feel Roxanne's presence any longer. In fact, it wasn't until that moment that she realized she'd felt her presence all along.

***

After everything had settled for the night and Addison convinced Luke to go home, she went up to her room. She'd thought about getting out the dress, but decided against it. It was late and she was tired. It could wait until tomorrow. In the hours that had passed, she hadn't felt Roxanne had returned. *What have I done?* She tossed and turned in bed for almost an hour before deciding to find out.

"Roxanne, are you there?" she whispered. "Can you hear me?"

Nothing.

She tried again.

"If you're here, please let me know."

Still nothing except the drip, drip, drip of a leaky bathroom faucet.

Addison tried a few more times, and, defeated, turned to the side and gave in to sleep.

CHAPTER 28

The air was crisp, the leaves just beginning to shake themselves free from the trees. Winter would soon blow through the sleepy town, leaving many to retreat to their homes for a season of hibernation. Unlike those who despised the cold, Addison welcomed it. The sting of winter's chill made her feel alive.

She followed the worn-down path behind her house and surveyed the area around her. It felt like she was playing a game of "I spy with my little eye" with herself. Ever since moving into the manor, she hadn't taken the time to breathe in her enchanted surroundings. Today with all the "what ifs" and "whys" swirling around in her head, the fresh air made her forget about it all.

Tree branches chipped and split beneath the pressure of the rubber tires on Addison's mountain bike. She wasn't sure where the path she'd taken would lead, or if it led anywhere at all, only that there was only one way to find out. An owl cooed above her. *Could it be the same one I heard the first day I was here?* She hoped so. She pictured it sitting majestically atop a tree, guiding her path from above.

A few minutes passed by. The owl sounded off again, this time more distant, farther away. But there was something else. A sound behind her. Footsteps? Another bike perhaps? She glanced back but saw nothing. The deeper she went into the woods, the quieter things were. Too quiet, as if everything was asleep. Where was all the wildlife? She'd expected to cross paths with all kinds of tiny creatures and had seen not a one.

The eerie silence circled around her. Then the sound came again, this time much louder than before. Addison stopped. This time she didn't turn around. She hopped off the bike and listened. She couldn't place what the sound was or even where it originated from, only that it reminded her of the *thump, thump, thump* of a slowing heartbeat.

"Is anyone there?"

No answer.

Maybe it's just an animal hiding, not wanting to show itself.

Whatever it was breathed. The breathing vibrated through the trees. It sounded human, except that it was too loud and too forceful, like a mythical giant in a fictional movie.

She spun around, canvassing the treetops, the ground. No one was there, and yet she could feel eyes on her. Watching. Waiting.

"Hello? Who's there?"

A whooping laugh followed—a loud, shrill kind of cackling.

Addison stood perfectly still, crippled by fear, contemplating her next move. When the sound came for a third time, she dropped the bike and did what came natural: she ran. She didn't know what she was running from, or who, and she didn't care.

Less than one minute into the sprint for home, she tripped, her shoelace catching on a twisted branch. She went down, the side of her cheek colliding with the rich earth below. And there she remained.

***

Addison didn't know how much time had passed when her eyes fluttered open again. She shoved a few fingers into her pocket, then pulled them out again, remembering she'd strapped her phone to her bike before she left.

The last thing she remembered was the sound of someone laughing. But what, or who? And why?

She sat up, spitting particles of damp soil onto the ground next to her. Her mouth was filled with it. The side of her cheek burned. She gently pressed a finger over the inflamed area and winced. She removed the finger and pulled it back, wiping a small amount of blood on her shirt. It had ripped in two places, a little blood wouldn't make things much worse.

The woods were quiet again. She heard no breathing, no laughing, nothing. She could see the roof of the manor from where she was sitting, but not her bike. Where was her bike? She couldn't remember.

The sturdy oak tree beside her offered enough support for her to rise to her knees. She caught her breath, then braced herself against it before trying to stand. She planted one foot flat on the ground and pushed up. Her body made little progress. It lifted and then sagged back down. She tried again, this time with more vigor. She shot up for a moment, hobbled around, then fell back to her knees again. She felt paralyzed, like someone had a hold of her head and was pressing down, keeping her there.

But that couldn't be. She was alone.

Out of breath, she leaned back against the tree. Low, melodic sounds could be heard in the distance. Someone was calling her name. She concentrated. A man shouted her name, followed by a second voice, also male. She recognized the first voice as Luke's, and breathed a sigh of relief. He knew where she'd gone, and she had no doubt he'd find her. The second voice was lower, fainter, not as easy to distinguish.

"I'm here," she called.

Neither replied. *Had they heard her?*

She didn't wait long for an answer. The next time Luke called out, he was close enough to see her hand hoisted high in the air, waving back and forth. When she was within his line of site he took one look at her and sprinted the rest of the way. The other man wasn't far behind, inhaling big gulps of air like his life depended on it. As Luke crouched at her side, she looked past him, anxious to identify the mysterious person who had trekked into the woods to find her.

A few moments later she could see him clearly and shook her head in disbelief.

CHAPTER 29

"Dad?"

Addison's father leaned over the side of the hospital bed and kissed her on the forehead.

"What…are…you…doing here?" Addison asked.

"I needed to talk to you."

"I thought you weren't coming again until next week."

"I couldn't wait."

She ran a hand through her dirt-filled hair. "I'm glad you're here."

He smiled. "Me too."

"It must be important if you came early," she said.

"What?"

"Whatever you have to tell me."

"It will keep until we get you home. I want the doctor to look at you first."

Addison's arm was broken. The doctor explained

she'd fallen on top of it when she tumbled to the ground. He rattled on using terms like "angulation" and "fracture," both words she had heard before but didn't quite understand. She stared blankly into his eyes, nodding. When he finished talking, he asked if she had any questions. She looked at her dad who then walked with the doctor out to the hallway, no doubt to make sure his every concern was satisfied.

The whole day had been a blur with only bits and pieces remaining in her memory. She tried to piece it all together, starting with the moment she'd left the house to find the bike path to when she woke up in the middle of the woods. The beginning and end were clear; it was the moments in-between she couldn't account for.

Her father returned to the room and explained they'd need to apply some type of cast to her arm before they could go.

"Where's Luke?" Addison asked.

"At the house. I drove you here. He asked me to call and give him an update. He's…umm…very nice."

"We're friends, Dad," she said, sitting up on the bed. "He's fixing up the house."

"I know. He told me."

She raised a brow. *What else has he told him?*

"What happened out there?" he asked.

In an attempt to quell his concerns, she said, "I tripped over something on the road. You know how clumsy I am sometimes." This was a fact that was more than a little true, earning her the nickname of "Butterfingers" by her aunt. If she didn't drop it, spill it, or lose it, she tripped over it.

"Why'd you leave your bike?"

Good question. She'd wondered that very thing herself. She handled the answer by pulling a switcheroo. "How long were you at the house before you found me?"

Her father leaned against the wall. "Oh, about fifteen minutes or so. Luke and I made our introductions, and he gave me a tour of the place. When you hadn't returned after we finished, we went looking for you."

Her dad's phone buzzed. He picked it up and looked at it. "Luke found your bike. He's such a nice young man."

"You said that already."

Her father winked. "He was so concerned about you; he carried you all the way back to the house. Looks like everything is going to be fine."

If only that were true.

***

Back at the house, Addison relaxed next to her father on the sofa. He'd let out a series of sighs over the last few minutes which were his "tells," something he did when he was getting ready to deliver news he didn't like giving. He'd sighed when she was five and her rabbit died. He'd sighed when she was twelve and he had to admit to cancelling the family vacation to Disneyland because of some last minute work thing. And most recently, he'd turned up at her old house, red-faced and sullen, dried tears staining his ruddy cheeks. He hadn't needed to speak then. She'd never seen him cry before, and she knew it meant something was wrong. Very wrong.

Addison was used to the sighing. Years of hearing it taught her the best thing to do was to wait. Eventually the heart of the matter would come out as it always did. The heavier the sigh, the heavier the confession. Today he was sighing harder than usual, a fact that she didn't want to let scare her, even though it did.

"I've come here," he began, "to tell you something that will come as a bit of a surprise to you."

She leaned back, as if understanding the magnitude of what he was about to say would be better received with as much calm as possible. He continued.

"When you were a child and your mother came to me and told me what you'd witnessed at your friend's house, I should have told you then that I believed you. I was wrong not to do that. And I'm sorry."

Although relieved, it was a bit of an odd confession to make after so much time had passed.

"Dad, is this because of what happened at dinner last time you were here? I haven't thought of it since then. If you have, then I'm the one who should be saying sorry. What I experienced as a kid…well…it was a long time ago. I know you never wanted to hurt me."

"I have thought of it. A great deal, actually. It's been bothering me ever since we parted company that night. When you told me the vision you had of Natalie wasn't the only one, I didn't want to believe it, even though I do."

"You…do?" She could barely speak the words. "Why? What changed?"

"You're my daughter. You've never said anything that wasn't true." He hunched over the arm of the couch with his back to her, his nervous gaze darting around like a bee without a flower to land on. Then he drew breath and let out the longest sigh of all. There was more.

"It means a lot to hear you believe me, even now," she said. "But that isn't what you came to tell me, is it?"

"I love you, Addy."

"I know, Dad."

She was just about to reach for him when he said, "Everything I've done has always been to protect you. You know that, right? You understand?"

His voice was shaky, uneven.

What was he saying—or *not* saying?

"You're scaring me," she said.

She patted him on the back with a hand. He wouldn't turn around. He seemed—afraid. But why? Not wanting to put it off any longer, she rose, walked over to him, and crouched before him. She took his hand and rubbed it gently. "Dad, you can tell me anything. It's okay. Please—whatever it is, won't you feel better once you get it out?"

"What I have to say will change everything. It will change the way you look at me. It might even change our relationship." He covered his eyes with an unsteady hand. "Oh, what am I saying? It will do all of those things."

Addison shook her head. "I don't believe that. Won't you at least look at me?"

After several moments, he slid his hand to the side. "No matter what happens, you have a right to know."

"What?"

"It's your grandmother, Addy."

She didn't understand. "What about her?"

"She's…alive."

CHAPTER 30

Addison tasted the salty wetness of her tears as they formed pools on her upper lip. It had been a long time since she'd had a good, hard cry. Even at her mother's funeral, she'd remained silent, keeping it all in, holding it together for her father. Now she let the tears flow. Not just for the news he'd given her, but for the loss of her mother too. For once in her life, she released it, letting it all go. Her father waited, his arm wrapped around her, his shoulder serving as a conduit for her to cry on.

Once she gathered herself together, she stood up, pacing the floor while shouting, "How?! How could you and Mom have lied to me for all these years?"

"We were trying to protect you."

She slammed a hand down on her jeans. "From what, Dad?! Maybe I didn't need protecting."

"If you knew the reasons—"

"Why you lied to me?" she asked. "Will hearing them

make it right?"

He shook his head. "I don't know. I'm trying to undo what's already been done in the best way I know how. Maybe you don't think parents are supposed to make mistakes, like we have some kind of child-raising handbook, and we can just whip it out, flip to a chapter, and see what we are supposed to do. We don't. It's trial and error. All of it is."

Her muscles tensed and her shoulder throbbed, the pain and stress flowing to one specific spot all at once. Her father had come clean. The least she could do is hear him out. She took a cleansing breath and sat back down. "I'm glad you told me. But I have questions, and I need answers."

He nodded, remaining silent.

"What made you decide to tell me?"

"A week ago I received a letter from Marjorie in the mail. Somehow she'd found out your mother had died. She begged me to let her see you, and knowing you were an adult now, she said if I didn't, she'd find you herself."

"So...you told me because you *had* to?"

"When I came here and we talked about the experiences you'd had as a child, I felt an overwhelming sense of guilt. I mulled it over on the plane ride home, all the while knowing if your mother was alive, she would never approve of me telling you. The last thing I wanted was to dishonor her memory by going against her wishes."

Addison crossed one leg over the other. "But you did it anyway."

"When I arrived home, I received another letter from your grandmother."

"What did it say?"

"That's what was strange. It was a piece of paper, folded several times, and when I opened it, there was only one sentence written in the middle of the page."

He reached into the pocket, pulled out a white piece of paper, and passed it to her. She turned it over in her hands before opening it. On the inside, written in all caps in red pen, it said: KEEP ADDISON AWAY FROM GRAYSON MANOR.

"She knows where you are, Addy. She knows you're here."

CHAPTER 31

Addison felt a shock stream through her system when she read the words scrawled on the paper. It was like someone had attached jumper cables to her body and pressed hard on the gas. She'd come to accept the fact that both of her grandparents knew the fate of Roxanne Rafferty and, for whatever reason, had chosen to cover it up. She'd tried searching for her grandfather and had almost given up. A man missing for that many years was probably an expert on how to stay missing.

She stared at her father. He stared back. "So you see," he said, palms up, "I had to tell you."

"Why would her knowing I'm here change your mind? Who cares what she says? By now she's a tired, ailing old woman."

"I wouldn't be so sure. I may not have seen her much, but one thing I remember—she was a force no one wanted to reckon with." He picked an envelope out of his pocket, unfolded it, and turned it around so the front of it faced her. "You see the return address? It says New York City."

"She's...here?"

"Well, not quite, but she's close enough."

"How long has she been here? What's she doing here? I don't understand."

His face looked grim. "Neither do I. Maybe she moved back to the area years ago—who knows. All I do know is—it's too close for comfort."

"Why didn't Mom want Marjorie to be in my life? Why keep her from me? What did she do that was so terrible?"

He held a hand out in front of him. "Slow down. I know you have a lot of questions. One at a time." He took a breath. "I'll start with the last. As you know, your mother was bounced around from place to place for years as a child. The older she got, the more she resented your grandmother for it. She despised her life after your grandfather left. I suppose even though he abandoned them, she blamed her mother for it. Who knows why? Your mother held that man up on a pedestal for reasons I never fully understood."

Addison did. The bond she shared with her own father was strong enough to withstand anything—even his most recent confession.

"As to your other question," he said, "about why your

mother kept Marjorie from you, it would be best if you let Marjorie explain."

Addison stared at her father—bewildered. "You say that like I'll be seeing her."

He looked away.

"Dad—what did you do?"

"The only thing I could do…I called her. I didn't want her getting to you before I did."

"What did you say?"

"I pleaded with her to let me talk to you first. I made a deal."

"In exchange for…?"

"Allowing her to meet you. You won't be alone. I'll be there."

Every possible emotion seemed to rush through her at once. "What if I don't want to see her?"

"You must. Now that your mother is gone, there are things about you that no one can explain but her. I know you're still looking for answers about the visions you had as a child. Marjorie can give them to you."

CHAPTER 32

When Luke walked through the front door to see if Addison needed anything, he found her lying flat on the couch, covered with a blanket, staring at the ceiling. "Where's your father?"

She propped herself up on one elbow and turned. "I put him in the bedroom next to mine upstairs."

"Do you think that's...safe? What if he gets a visit from a not-so-friendly ghost? How are you going to explain?"

She shook her head. "I honestly don't know. He's determined to stay here until after I've seen my grandmother."

"Wait a minute, isn't she—"

"Dead?" Addison finished for him. "Apparently not."

She relayed the conversation she had with her father earlier.

"And the weird gets weirder," he said when she'd

finished. "You nervous to meet her?"

She sat up. "I don't know what I am right now."

He sat down beside her. "What happened out there in the woods? Why weren't you with your bike when I found you?"

"I have no idea. I keep thinking about it. I remember leaving the house. I could hear an owl somewhere nearby. I was following the trail, even though I had no idea where it would lead. Then I woke up with bruises, scratches, and a broken arm. I tried to stand up. I couldn't."

"Maybe you *shouldn't* think about it."

"What are you saying?"

"In my experience, when you let go of something, that's when it comes back to you. The harder you try to force yourself to remember, the bigger the resistance."

"I'll try that," she said. "I need to get cleaned up anyway."

"Why?"

"I imagine I look—"

"Beautiful," he said. "You look beautiful."

Her cell phone rang, breaking the awkward silence between them.

"Is this Addison Lockhart?" said a female voice on the other end.

The woman on the other end of the line verified herself as Detective Ross.

"Are you calling about the dress?" Addison asked. "I can bring it in tomorrow if that's okay."

"Dress?"

"Yes. I'd like to stay while it's tested. I'd rather not come home without it." Addison knew it was a stretch. She didn't know if the results would take hours or days, and if blood *was* found on the dress, there was little chance she'd get it back—ever. That meant if she was going to touch it again, it had to be now. But how, with her father next door? There was no guarantee what might happen. It was a risk, but at this point, it was one she was willing to take.

"What dress?" the detective asked, again.

"I'm sorry—you're calling about something else?"

"I heard you were trying to get in touch with the men who worked the Roxanne Rafferty case."

"I don't understand? He was already here. He came yesterday."

"Who?" Detective Ross asked.

"Detective Houston."

Another pause. "Ma'am, Detective Houston died several years ago."

It wasn't possible.

"Are you sure you have the names right?"

Addison heard a shuffling sound in the background. "I've got the paperwork here. Says Detective Houston is dead and Dobbs is in a wheelchair at Mortimer

Retirement Home."

"The man who came here walked around my house and talked to me about what he remembered when he worked the case."

"Ma'am, listen to me carefully. Dobbs is the only one still alive, and he has Alzheimer's. So, it wasn't him. Whoever came to your house isn't who he says he is. I'd like you to come in and fill out a police report."

The phone slipped from Addison's hands in front of a confused Luke, who watched it fall to the floor, the screen shattering.

"What is it? What's wrong?" he asked.

Addison turned and raced up the stairs, not stopping until she reached her room. She reached for the box beneath her bed, relieved when she found it. Luke followed close behind. "Addison, what's going on?"

She lifted the lid. The dress was gone.

CHAPTER 33

Addison and Luke slipped out of the house carefully and quietly so they wouldn't wake her father. He had a nightly ritual of being to bed by eight and getting up before the sun rose, around four or five. She placed a quick return call to the police station using Luke's phone, letting Detective Ross know she'd accidentally dropped her phone and that everything was all right—though she felt far from it.

"Where are we going again?" Luke asked.

"It's called Mortimer Retirement Home. I looked it up. It's right here in Rhinebeck."

Luke punched the address into the GPS. "Isn't it a bit late to be going there?"

"I need to do *something*—I'm about to lose my mind. I wish I knew who that man really was...he must have stolen the dress."

"How'd he even manage to get it out of there?" Luke

asked.

"I left him alone in my bedroom for about thirty seconds when you arrived," Addison said. "He was carrying that prehistoric briefcase around. He must have shoved it in there.

"And we stood outside and watched him drive away with it."

She thought of the car he was in, a gold sedan. It looked like a Lexus, but she couldn't be sure.

They pulled into the parking lot at the retirement home and parked. "What's your plan?" he asked.

"For what?"

"You can't just walk in here and expect to talk to the guy. In some of these places you can't even visit a person unless you're on the naughty or nice list."

She laughed. "What if I'm on neither?"

A plan was hatched for Luke to distract whoever was working at the front desk while Addison found Dobbs's room. It turned out their last minute plotting wasn't necessary. No one was manning the station at the front desk or anywhere around there—that is, until Addison rounded the corner. She quickly backpedaled. "Someone's coming."

Luke pushed her into the ladies room. "Wait one minute, then come out. Try to act natural," he said in a loud whisper.

As opposed to what? She hadn't felt "natural" for

years. The seconds ticked by slower than usual, it seemed. After the minute was over, she cracked the door open, peeking out at the woman engaged in a friendly back-and-forth banter with Luke. The woman couldn't take her eyes off of him, which is exactly what Addison thought she wanted, until the woman laid a playful hand on his arm. Addison couldn't tear her eyes away from the woman's sparkly green fingernails—they were like little daggers. One touch, then another. Luke played it cool, leaning over the desk and directing the woman's attention to something on the opposite end of the room. For a brief moment he turned, his eyes enlarged as if to say: What are you waiting for?

Addison slipped out and made it around the corner, resisting the urge to back up and sneak another glance at Green Glitter Lady. She was there for one reason, she reminded herself. Nothing else mattered. Not even her. The corridor wound around in a square shape like a wraparound porch with rooms lining the left side. Addison expected name plates on each door. There was nothing. No way to discern who occupied the various apartments. Now what?

A woman with curly, silver hair that looked like it had been dipped in light purple food coloring opened her door and looked out. Addison hadn't heard the door open. The woman said, "*Psst...*" Addison turned.

"Visiting hours ended at seven o'clock," the woman

said.

Addison frowned. "I didn't know. This is my first time."

"What are you doing here?" the woman demanded.

"Looking for someone."

"Who?"

In that moment, Addison realized something. She didn't know Dobbs's first name. "My name is Addison Dobbs."

"Patricia York. What do you want with Hector?"

"He's my, umm, uncle."

"You're looking for Hector?"

"Do you know which apartment is his?"

Patricia bit her upper lip and then scratched her head with her finger. She wouldn't give the room number up that easily.

"I've been told he has Alzheimer's."

She offered a slow nod. "It's moderate. He can't read or write anymore. Most times when I see him he's staring at things like he's trying to remember what they are."

"Have you been here long?"

"Going on five years now. Hector was here when I arrived. Of course he wasn't as bad back then. He had some difficulty talking, but he hadn't been diagnosed yet." Patricia made a swooping motion with her hand. "Come here a moment, and be quiet about it."

As if Addison's goal was to wake every resident on

the first floor.

She moved closer.

"Keep coming," Patricia prompted.

Addison felt like a mouse entranced by a piece of cheese. When she was within two feet of her, Patricia stepped forward. "Hector doesn't get visitors. Not anymore. And he never said anything to me about having a niece. Not one your age. Who are you *really?*"

Addison panicked.

"The best thing you can do is tell the truth now," Patricia said. "I suspect you know that. You have a sweet face, and I truly believe you don't want to lie to me, but don't try it again."

Obviously the retirement home had a neighborhood watch in the form of this sprightly, curious woman. Addison confessed, telling Patricia only what she thought she needed to know. She explained Detective Dobbs had once worked a case involving a missing woman, and Addison had reason to believe after all this time, that the case might be able to be solved. She left out the part about the spirit of Roxanne Rafferty. The woman didn't seem to remember who Roxanne was, but she knew all about the career of Hector Dobbs, saying she'd spent many hours when they first met listening to his exciting stories. Something in Patricia's voice led Addison to believe she had wanted more than just friendship with him at one time, so naturally she'd be protective of

Hector. Even now.

After Addison explained her reason for being there, Patricia said something unexpected. "If I tell you where he is, will you come back?"

"When I've finished talking to him?" Addison asked. "I don't know if that's a good idea. I'm already not supposed to be—"

"Another day. You're good at telling stories. I could use more entertainment in my life." Without waiting for Addison to respond, she added, "Room 77A, around the corner, third room on your left." She walked out into the hall and looked left and then right as if she was part of Addison's covert operation. "What are you waiting for? You better get going."

Thinking Patricia had intentions on accompanying her, Addison said, "Aren't you supposed to be in your apartment?"

The woman giggled. "No dear, I'm not a resident. I work here."

***

Former Detective Hector Dobbs stared out his bedroom window and into the dark blackness of night. He had a few patches of stringy hair left on his nearly bald head, and even though he was seated, Addison could tell he was a lot shorter than she imagined he'd be. A rancid smell permeated the room, compelling her to cup a hand over her nose when she breathed.

She had never been around anyone with Alzheimer's before and had no idea what to expect. She uttered a barely audible "hello" when she walked in, doing her best not to startle him. He glanced back, gave her a look like he had little to no interest in why she was there, and then gazed back out the window again.

Does he think I'm the help?

If he did, maybe it was a good thing. The last thing she wanted was for him to make enough noise to summon the real help.

She walked over and knelt in front of him so her face was eye level with his. "Hi Mr. Dobbs. I'm new here. Can I get you anything?"

Hector shriveled his face up in such a way that she got the message—he considered her a nuisance. He didn't want her there. He crossed his arms over his body, wrapping his hands around them like he was trying to protect himself.

"Are you cold—do you need a blanket?" she asked.

He grunted. She couldn't decipher the intention of the grunt. She grabbed a blanket from the bed and laid it over him. It fell to a puddle on the floor. Hector tilted his head to the side, his eyes glazed over. It hung there like he didn't have the will or the energy to prop it back up again. This man was probably a formidable detective in his day, and the image of him now saddened her.

"I heard you used to be a great detective."

What was she thinking? Clearly his lights upstairs had been off for a long time. She slumped to the floor, muttering to herself. "I wish you could talk to me. You might be the only one who can help me. You worked on a case a long time ago. A young actress, Roxanne Rafferty, disappeared in the fifties. No one ever found out what happened to her. I thought you might know something. That's why I came here tonight. I think someone killed her. Someone right here in this town or in this city. And I don't know why. All I know is I can't prove it, and I don't know where else to turn." She glanced up at him. There was no change. "I'm sorry I bothered you, Mr. Dobbs, and I'm even sorrier for what's become of you. You don't deserve this. No one does."

With one swoop of his hand, he reached forward, narrowly missing Addison, and toppled over in the process. His body smacked on the ground with a large thud. Shocked, Addison bent to her knees, clutching onto him with the one good arm she had left. It took several attempts to help him off the floor. When she got him to his feet, she slung her uninjured arm around him. Together, they walked over to the bed. She lifted the covers and he dropped down like an oversized sack of flour.

"I never meant for this to happen. I shouldn't have come. I'll leave now." She didn't know why, but she bent down and hugged him. Somehow she knew he needed it.

Hector reached out again. He placed both hands on her arms and squeezed. "Gray...Gray...Grayson Manor," he stammered.

Addison nodded. "Yes, Grayson Manor. That's where I live."

An intense look of trepidation showed in his eyes. His head swiveled back and forth uncontrollably.

"What is it? What's wrong?" she asked.

"She."

"She who? Roxanne?"

"She...murdered."

CHAPTER 34

Addison attempted to elicit more information from Hector, but once he'd uttered those two little words, he fell back into a dazed stupor. Nothing Addison did or said could shake him out of it. She slipped out a side door and met Luke at the car, their chosen rendezvous point.

"*She murdered?* What do you suppose that means?" Luke asked.

"Who knows—at his point, it could mean everything or it could mean nothing. Hector was completely out of it. I'm surprised he said anything."

"So you don't believe he was trying to tell you something?"

Addison drew a long breath. "I'm not sure."

"What if he knew something? Something he couldn't prove."

"Like what?"

"Maybe he was trying to tell you Roxanne was

murdered by a woman."

"Or maybe he was saying she *was* murdered. He said *she*, paused, then said *murdered*. A man stole the dress, not a woman."

"What about Marjorie? You still going to see her tomorrow?" he asked.

She nodded.

"I don't like it. You know nothing about her, and you don't owe her anything."

It was the first time she'd ever heard him raise his voice. It was lower, deeper; he wasn't exactly yelling, but he managed to get his message across all the same.

"My father said she knows things about me. Maybe she can tell me why I see things. I have to find out."

"You said yourself, he never really knew her. It could be a trap. I don't care how old she is."

She looked at him, knowing he might be right. But it was something she had to do.

***

That night Addison had a dream. She was back on the wooded path she'd been on the day before. This time, she wasn't on her bike, and she wasn't walking. She wasn't even on the ground. She was high up in a tree, so high she didn't know how she got there. She felt light and airy, weightless. The branch she sat on was thin, too small to hold her. So why wasn't she falling?

She looked around. What she saw shocked her. Even though it was dark, she had a strange kind of binocular vision. It was similar to her own, but different. She could turn her head, but her eyes didn't move in their sockets. On the ground below her, she saw a person lying on the ground. A woman. She wasn't moving. Not at first.

A few minutes passed. The woman began to tremble like she'd been left out in the cold. Only it wasn't cold. Addison felt warm inside. The woman's eyes flashed open. She looked around. She looked up. She looked at Addison. She *was* Addison.

It isn't possible. How can I be in the tree and on the ground at the same time?

She stared at the mirror image of herself in disbelief.

What's happening?

The Addison on the ground tried to sit up, a feat she didn't conquer at first. She pressed one hand against the ground, forcing herself to a sitting position. She took the same hand and rubbed her arm. *The same arm that was bandaged later that day.* She braced against the tree and tried to stand. It didn't work. Frustrated, she pressed both hands flat on the ground. And that's when the Addison in the tree saw something she couldn't believe: a bright light. The area surrounding her counterpart on the ground lit up like a full moon on a clear night.

CHAPTER 35

Addison bolted up in bed and ran a hand across her comforter, feeling around for her cell phone. She grabbed it and dialed Luke's number. "How fast can you get here?"

"I'm on my way now," he responded. "What's wrong?"

The bathroom shower knob down the hall squeaked and then switched off. "I'll meet you outside. Don't come in when you get here."

She pressed the end button on her phone and glanced around the room, selecting a worn-out pair of rubber-soled slippers and a coral zip-up sweatshirt. She thought about grabbing her jacket. There wasn't time. She stepped into the hall just as her dad exited the bathroom, dressed and ready for the day. Their eyes met. He looked her up and down. "Where are you off to dressed in your PJs?"

"I was looking for something. I think I left it in my car."

"Let me get it for you," he said. "I was just going downstairs anyway."

"That's all right, Dad," she called, already halfway down the stairs. "It'll only take a minute."

Luke's truck lulled to a stop a minute later. Addison was outside standing next to her car, waiting. He exited the truck, leaving the door open. "What's going on?" he asked. "Did you see something last night?"

"Yes and no. I didn't see Roxanne, but I saw something else."

"What? Where?"

"In a dream."

Luke crossed his arms in front of him. "I'm listening."

"I was up in this tree, and here's the crazy part—I think I was an…"

She hesitated, considering how lame she would feel when she said it out loud. It didn't matter. She had to.

"A what?" Luke asked.

Even though it was cool outside, Addison felt her cheeks increase in temperature. "An…owl."

The fifteen-second silence between them seemed to stretch into eternity until Luke laughed. And not just any laugh—the kind that started deep down inside someone's gut. "What was that like?"

"I have no idea. I didn't even realize I wasn't in my

own body until I tried to move my eyes. They wouldn't move. It was like they couldn't. My head swiveled though, and I could see what was happening on the ground."

"What was going on?"

"I saw myself."

"I thought you were in the tree?"

She huffed at him, frustrated. "It was a dream. Do yours always make sense?"

He shrugged. "Go on."

"It's like I was two people. The first was in the form of an owl, looking down from a branch on the tree. The second was my physical body lying on the ground in the exact spot where I tripped and fell yesterday."

"Did you remember anything?"

"I remembered everything. The whole experience came rushing back to me all at once."

"So...what happened?"

"The ground where I fell was glowing. It was like light had reflected off the sun and beamed its rays right on the spot I sat in. Only, I wasn't aware of it—I mean, the me on the ground wasn't aware of it. And there's no way I could have missed it. It was the brightest light I'd ever seen, uh, me the owl."

Luke opened his mouth to reply and at the same time, Addison's front door opened. Her dad stepped out. "What are you two doing out here?"

She glared at Luke who stared at her father. "Mind if I borrow your daughter for a minute?" he asked.

The request seemed to please her father very much. He waved both hands in front of him. "Don't mind me. I'll see you two...well...whenever I see you. Take your time." Grinning, her dad walked back inside the house.

"You were saying?" Luke said.

"I was telling you about the light."

"Is it possible whatever memory you had was somehow magnified—like whatever happened didn't actually happen? In the dream you were an owl, and obviously that's not true." He winked. "Or is there something else you haven't told me about?"

She shoved him. "I'm being serious."

"So am I," he joked.

"To me, the owl in the tree represented something I needed to see."

"Which means?"

Addison leaned in close. "Do you have a shovel?"

CHAPTER 36

Luke had many items in the long toolboxes in the back of his pickup. A shovel was not one of them. He walked with Addison back to the place she had fallen, and they both surveyed the area. It looked plain and ordinary, almost like nothing had happened in that spot since the day the soil settled on the ground.

A plan was made. Addison and her father would go meet Marjorie. In the meantime, Luke would return with a shovel and do some blind-faith digging. She was perplexed at his continued belief in her. He didn't question it, he didn't doubt it; he just went to work.

An hour later Addison was behind the wheel of the car she purchased when she arrived in New York, a Mazda MX-5 Miata convertible. She'd always wanted a convertible. When she'd taken it for a spin during the test drive, the reedy salesman made his pitch, enunciating the words "liquid silver," as if the color gave the car special power. Either way, she couldn't resist. Her father, on the other hand, seemed ill at ease inside the small two-seater. With one hand, he gripped the side of his seat. With the other, he took hold of the door handle like it was some kind of emergency safety latch he could pull in case of an emergency evacuation. To put his daughter at ease, he whistled the tune of an old Beatles song, soft and low, acting like nothing at all was the matter. She wasn't fooled. It was another thing he did when he was nervous.

The more she thought about it, the more odd quirks her father seemed to have. She wondered if he was even aware of them, or if they were like a window into his soul that only others could see. She'd heard about something like this on her first day of college and hadn't ever forgotten it. The speaker had said everyone had parts of themselves only others could see. How many did she have yet to recognize about herself?

The address Marjorie had given Addison's father was 1051 Delancey Street. It was at this exact spot that she realized something was wrong. The structure at 1051 Delancey Street wasn't a house, a condominium, or even a high-rise apartment building. It was a mom and pop coffee shop that also served soup, something Addison considered to be a unique combination.

"This can't be right," she said, driving past the coffee shop and turning around.

Her father stretched a yellow Post-it note out in front of her. "See?" he said. "'Fraid it is."

"Do you think she gave you the wrong address on accident or on purpose?"

"I can't see why she'd lie about it—she seemed determined to meet you." He shrugged. "I can try the phone number she gave me." He dialed the number. It rang. No one answered.

"What are we supposed to do now?" Addison groaned.

Her father smiled. "Well, we're here. Let's go in and get some coffee."

She didn't want coffee. She wanted answers. Something she wasn't likely to get.

They parked the car and crossed the street together. Addison stopped in front of the coffee shop and sent a text message to Luke on a phone he loaned her, asking if he'd found anything. His reply? *Not yet.* The entire day was turning out to be a bust.

The coffee house/soup kitchen was buzzing, mostly with a wide variety of twenty-somethings who *tap, tap, tapped* on the keyboards of their laptops while sipping various forms of pricey frappes. Not one soul in the entire joint looked up when they walked in. No one could be bothered with what anyone else was doing; they were too involved in their own affairs to care. A boy in the far corner wearing a burnout T-shirt and a YOLO cap swirled his head around in the air like Stevie Wonder. The tabletop served as his piano, and his cup as the microphone. With his eyes seamed shut, he lip-synched the tune to whatever was blaring through the black Beats by Dre headphones he wore on his ears.

"He seems happy," her father laughed, bending a finger in the boy's direction.

They ordered and sat down. Addison was too disappointed to order. Her father, on the other hand, was perfectly content with his special-of-the-day, mint-flavored coffee the lady behind the counter said tasted like the popular cookies the Girl Scouts made each year.

"We wasted our time coming here, expecting to find her. I thought she always wanted to be in my life. What a joke."

He took a sip of his drink and then quickly set it down. "It's far too sweet for me. You want to try it?"

She shook her head. She wanted to leave, but couldn't. She was waiting for Luke to text her to let her know what he found or didn't find. Until then, she was to keep her father occupied. She sat back, seriously considering ordering a bowl of soup, when the door made a dinging sound to indicate another customer had entered.

Unlike the other self-absorbed patrons, Addison *did* look up and watched her grandmother walk inside. Well, not walked as much as waltzed, the way one did when they expected all eyes to be on them—even after all these years. They weren't, though she didn't notice. Even in a slenderizing pair of jeans and a zipped-up, nylon windbreaker, she crossed the room with grace and elegance. Even without the fur coat or the heeled shoes, one thing hadn't changed: her lips. They were still painted a deep shade of red. She looked left, then right, lined Addison up in her sights like a hunter aiming his rifle, and charged.

"You look like me," Marjorie said when she reached the table. "Did you know that before now?"

Whatever happened to "hello" or "nice to see you after all this time" or "I'm so glad to finally meet you."?

"Hello Marjorie," her father said.

"Bill," Marjorie answered without even glancing in his direction. "A moment, if you please."

"With me?" Addison asked.

"Of course," Marjorie replied. "But first," she said, finally setting eyes on Addison's father, "there's a bookshop around the corner. Could you occupy yourself there for a while? I need to speak with my granddaughter alone. You understand why. I expect this is not a problem?"

He stood up like a wind-up robot. Addison blinked in disbelief. At first he looked like he was going to comply without even giving a response. Then he said, "After I've had my say."

"Dad," Addison said, grabbing his arm. She looked at him as if to say: *You're not going to leave me alone with her.*

He leaned down and whispered into her ear. "Don't worry. I'll be watching." He tapped the flap of his pants pocket with his hand just enough for her to see something was inside. Binoculars?

An impatient Marjorie rolled her eyes and flicked her hand toward the door. "Let's get on with it."

The two of them walked outside. What followed was like watching a bizarre movie scene with an unseen twist. What was going on? And why was he doing exactly as she asked? What's more—why had Marjorie put the coffee shop as her address?

The banter between father and grandmother went on for several minutes. They both looked irritated. They bickered, neither relenting at first until her father nodded, then sighed. Not a good sign. He then turned and walked away. *What did he know that she didn't?*

Marjorie walked back in, placed a flat hand on both sides of Addison's cheeks, and smiled. "At long last. Now then, I'm sure you have a lot of questions. Get them out of your system so we can discuss the real reason you're here."

"Why did you choose a coffee shop?"

"I'll explain later. Next question."

Addison wasn't satisfied. And unlike her father, she

wasn't about to let up. "Why couldn't we meet at your house? Do you even have one? Do you live here?"

Marjorie removed the grey, leather gloves from her hands and flopped them down on the table. "Is this really what you want to ask me? I hoped for so much more. How disappointing."

Addison leaned back in the chair and folded her hands over her lap, unsure of what to say next. Did she dare ask?

The prolonged silence didn't suit Marjorie's personality. She locked eyes with Addison. "How long have you lived in the manor?"

"How did you know I was there?"

She snickered the way a person did when they were privy to something the other person couldn't possibly understand. "I could see you coming."

"What do you mean—*see me*? You saw us in the car when we were parking?"

She shook her head. "No, dearest, I saw you in my mind. You really don't know anything, do you?"

CHAPTER 37

Addison's grandmother leaned forward, waiting for an answer.

"I haven't lived there long," Addison said.

"I never thought you'd actually be interested in the place, or I would have never allowed your mother to leave it to you in her will."

"You assume a lot for someone who doesn't know me."

"I suppose you're right, but knowing your mother, I assumed she would steer you clear of the place."

Addison folded her arms and rested them on the edge of the table. "Why?"

"Bad memories."

"What happened to make her feel that way?"

Her grandmother clacked her fingernails along the table's surface, well aware of the little song and dance routine they were playing with each other. "I want you to leave that house immediately."

Addison's jaw tightened. "No."

"It isn't a request."

"The house was deeded to me, and I intend to stay there. It doesn't belong to you anymore."

"You have no idea the kind of danger you're putting yourself in, child."

"If there's something I need to know, why don't you tell me?"

"Such a defiant little thing, aren't you? I see your mother raised you well. All right then, if it's truth you want, it's truth you shall have. Let's talk about your gift. And don't bother denying it; I know you're using it."

"How?"

"Answer my questions, and I'll answer yours."

Addison slumped back in the chair. She barely knew her grandmother, and here she was asking her to reveal things she didn't even share with those closest to her. And yet her grandmother *knew* things. Addison could tell. It was like she knew what Addison was going to say before she said it.

"I haven't got all day," Marjorie said. "So let's get things rolling, shall we? Do you know what a medium is?"

"Someone who sees spirits?"

"And communicates with them. What happened when you were five?"

"What do you mean?"

"You saw something—what was it?"

How does she know about the birthday party? My dad wouldn't have told her, would he?

"I…I…was at a birthday party." She couldn't believe she was actually saying it.

"Go on," Marjorie prompted.

"My friend Natalie's hair bow fell out. I picked it up."

"And what did you see?"

"Natalie. On the swing. She was soaring, swinging so high. The rope on the swing snapped, and she fell. Somehow I knew she wasn't going to be all right. I knew, even then, that within days she'd be dead."

"And when it happened, did she die?"

Addison hung her head and nodded.

"How did it make you feel?"

"Like I could have saved her, if only…"

"If only, what?"

"Someone would have believed me."

"But no one did, did they?"

Addison shook her head, ashamed.

Marjorie reached her hand across the table, resting it gently on Addison's arm. "I believe you."

"Why?"

"Because I see things too…just like my mother before me, and just like your mother before you."

"It's not possible. My mother—"

Marjorie lifted a finger to Addison's lips. "It's my turn now. I'm going to tell you a story. I'd like you to listen carefully and not to interrupt until I've finished. There will be plenty of time for questions later."

The words that followed were the unfiltered truth: Addison was a medium. It was a gift bestowed upon every firstborn daughter over the past several generations when they turned five. By the use of touch, the medium could receive visions pertaining to the past or the future. Once that was mastered and the medium's belief in her power grew stronger, she could use her hands for all kinds of things, and if her hands were used together, she could draw upon things even more vividly. Addison thought back to the dream she'd had of seeing herself in the woods, hands pressed firmly into the rich terra firma, the ground around her erupting with light. It had been her gift shining through, showing her the way.

Marjorie explained that for the gift to pass from mother to child, one thing needed to happen: the child needed to believe, and the mother needed to nurture that belief, helping her daughter to accept the gift and teaching her how to use it. When this happened, the gift transferred, gradually at first, until the mother no longer had it. Such was the case between Marjorie and Addison's mother, who didn't want to believe. When she turned five, the nurturing process began. Then something happened. An event, but Marjorie wouldn't go into detail. She didn't need to—Addison knew exactly what it was.

"What happened when my mother rejected her gift?" Addison probed.

"She didn't reject it exactly. She became angry with something she saw. She looked me in the eye and swore that one day when she grew up and had a child of her own, she'd never allow the child to have the gift. She didn't see it as good; she thought it was evil. But it's not evil at all."

"Is that why she kept you away from me?"

Marjorie fidgeted in her chair. "Mostly. I was hoping I could reason with her—help her understand the significance of what she was doing. When she refused to accept it, the gift remained with me, waiting to be passed on to the next generation, to my granddaughter. You see, if I die without passing it on, it dies with me."

"Did my mother understand this?"

"She didn't care. Stubborn girl. Always was." Marjorie glanced out the window and squinted, like she saw something.

"What is it?"

"Nothing." She lifted a finger and pointed at Addison. "A couple of weeks ago you saw something that made you believe again."

"How did you know about that?"

"I felt it, and every time you've experienced any type

of vision since, I've felt those too."

"Can you see what I'm seeing?"

Marjorie shook her head. "It doesn't work like that. The more you use it, the more *you* see, and the less I do. Yesterday you really believed, for the first time. You may have thought you did before that, but you still had your doubts. You have more power in your hands than you know, and it won't be long now until everything I possess is inside of you."

It pained Addison to reflect back on the way her mother had reacted when she tried to tell her what she saw. Nothing in her facial expressions offered even the slightest hint that she knew her daughter was telling the truth. Her mother had understood what was happening to her, and yet she'd done nothing to help her little girl. Addison didn't know whether to laugh, cry, to place blame, or to combine them all into one, big emotional tirade. "I want to know what happened to my mother as a child."

Marjorie jerked her head back, as if shocked by Addison's frankness. "Certainly not."

Addison wasn't dissuaded. She'd come this far—she wasn't leaving without some answers. In a hushed tone, she said, "Then tell me what happened to Roxanne Rafferty. And where's my grandfather?"

"What do you *think* you've seen?"

"I don't *think* anything—I know. And so do you.

That's partly why you're here, isn't it—to warn me—to scare me away?"

"Your visions aren't always as accurate as they seem," Marjorie argued. "You won't understand them fully until I've had the chance to work with you."

"What I saw...it was...very real."

"I'm sure it was. Now let me explain—"

"The only explanation I'm looking for right now is for you to tell me who killed Roxanne, why, and where I can find her body."

Marjorie held her gaze, unfettered. "What do *you* think happened? You've obviously seen something, so let's hear it."

"I found the dress."

"What dress?"

"The one in the hidden room. It was old and stained with blood."

"You're sure it was blood?"

"I was going to have it tested, but then something happened."

"What?"

"A man came over. He said he was a detective and had once worked on the case. I found out later that he'd lied. The department said that detective had died years ago, and when I opened the box, the dress was gone."

There was no denying the concern displayed on Marjorie's face. What Addison said worried her. "What did he look like—the man?"

"He was older, grey hair, beard. He had an old briefcase with him—I think he must have stuffed the dress inside of it to get it out of the house."

"Have you seen him again?"

Addison shook her head.

Without warning, Marjorie shot out of her chair, grabbing the gloves with one hand and Addison's wrist with the other. "We must go. Now."

"What—why?"

"Someone is watching."

When they reached the door, Marjorie released her grip on Addison and said, "I want you to leave the manor. Promise me. It isn't safe for you there."

They walked outside. Addison's father was sitting on a bench outside, waiting. She waved him over and then turned back to her grandmother. She was gone.

CHAPTER 38

"How could you leave me in there alone with that...that woman?!" Addison said to her father.

"You needed to learn about your history, Addison. I only wish I'd done it sooner. Where is she?"

Addison shrugged. "She took off once we got outside. Didn't you see her? She said someone was watching."

"What do you mean, *watching*?"

Addison's shoulders rose, then fell. "I have no idea."

"She didn't say who?"

"We never got that far. Whoever it was spooked her. Up until that moment, she'd been smug, cold almost. Then her whole demeanor changed."

"Your mother always said Marjorie wasn't big on sweet sentiments."

As they crossed the street, Addison looked around. A man in a funny black hat glared at her as he walked by. A woman smacked into her shoulder. People were everywhere. It was New York City for heaven's sake. There was no way she'd be able to decipher the difference between an average person and a stalker, if that's who they were dealing with.

"I need to tell you something," Addison said when she started the car, "and you're not going to like it. Marjorie told me to leave the manor again just now. She said it wasn't safe."

He had a confused look on his face. "Did you find out why she keeps saying that? Seems like a nice place to me."

She looked at her father and frowned. "I think Mom saw something she wasn't meant to when she was a child. I tried asking Marjorie, but she wouldn't budge."

Her father tapped a finger on the dashboard of the car. "Like what?"

"You let me meet her today because you know, don't you? You know about my gift."

He bowed his head and nodded.

"I haven't had a vision in a very long time, but when I moved to Grayson Manor, it started again." Over the next several minutes she did her best to explain what had occurred since she moved to the manor, giving him minor details, hoping this time he would understand.

"I never should have let you feel I didn't believe you. I see that now and I'm sorry."

Addison reached out and patted him on the arm, "No

one is perfect, Dad. And it's okay. You don't have to keep apologizing over and over. I know why you did it. I just can't believe after everything, you'd want me anywhere around Marjorie. She seems like such an ice cold person to me."

He sighed.

Here it comes.

"There's something you don't know. After your mother told me what you could do…well…see, and I'd seen proof of it, I called Marjorie. Your mother never knew about this call. Marjorie may not be the kindest woman I've ever met, but she helped me make sense of something your mother refused to discuss in detail with me. At the end of our conversation she only asked for one thing."

"What was it?"

"That one day when the time was right, I'd let her see you again."

CHAPTER 39

An eerie stillness filled the air when Addison and her father arrived home. Luke's truck was parked out front, but there was no sign of him anywhere. She dialed his number. It went straight to voicemail. She shouted his name. Her father shouted his name. A deadly quiet followed.

"We need to check the woods," Addison said.

Her father looked at her, perplexed.

"I'll explain later. Hurry!"

He frowned. "Addison, what's going on? How do you know Luke is out there? And don't say you'll tell me later. I want to know *now.*"

"He was looking for something," she replied. But she wasn't looking at him.

"What?"

The knot in Addison's throat enlarged, first feeling like a ping-pong ball and then expanding a few sizes.

She pressed a hand against her throat and tried to breathe. "I…can't…explain…right…now," she stammered. "I'm sorry, Dad. But I have to get to him." She began to run. She felt guilty for leaving her father behind, but she had to; something didn't feel right. And, when she reached a half-dug hole in the ground, and saw the limp, lifeless body lying inside of it, she knew why. She collapsed to the ground, pressing two fingers to the side of Luke's neck. She'd hoped to feel signs of life. What she experienced was something else entirely.

***

In her vision, the area surrounding Luke was sheathed in a fog-like haze. He stood over the area Addison had been found in and chucked piles of debris over his shoulder with the shovel, sprinkling dirt onto the ground below. He dug a few feet down and peered inside, like he'd noticed something. Addison couldn't see what it was—she could only see him, not inside the hole.

He leaned the shovel against the tree and lowered his head into the area he'd just excavated. He reached a hand in and pulled out a small object, turning it over in his hand to inspect it. After he'd stared at it for several seconds, he held it up to the light and then gasped, gently setting it down next to him before dropping himself back into the hole again. Both of his hands were hard at work now, shovel tossed to the side, as he clawed his way deeper into the hole. Addison shifted her gaze to the object he'd set to the side. It was a bone, and it looked like a human's.

The sound of footsteps approached, but Luke didn't seem to notice. A hand reached through the mist, picked up the shovel, and whacked Luke on the back of the head. He slumped over, falling into the hole. His cell phone flung through the air and landed several feet away. She turned again, determined to see the face of the person holding the shovel. He was gone. Running. He was running away. Why was this person running away when there was no one else here?

Addison's father's voice penetrated her vision. He was yelling her name. She felt her body being tossed around violently like it had gone limp. Her father grabbed her hand, pulling it off Luke. When she opened her eyes, her father was hunched over her, his face crippled with fear. She reached out a hand and cupped it around his cheek. "I'm fine, Dad," she said. "We have to get Luke to the hospital."

"Is he…alive?"

Addison wasn't sure. She leaned in and touched him once more. This time, she was on the beach overlooking the sea. Luke stood across from her. He looked different somehow, older, and his hair was shorter. He was smiling. She was smiling. And she felt an overwhelming sense of peace. As she looked around, she realized they weren't alone. People were gathered around. Some she recognized, others she didn't. One woman in particular stood out, grinning at Addison like they were best friends. She saw her father, and Luke's parents, and three girls she'd never seen before wearing what appeared to be the same exact dress. *The same dress? That only happens at a...* She turned her attention back to the mirror image of herself, now noticing she was also wearing a dress. But it wasn't white. It was a soft, pink color with spaghetti straps and a corseted bodice. Luke was in a fitted grey suit with the bottoms of his pant legs rolled up. She glanced down. Neither of them was wearing shoes; instead their feet dug into the sand. A man stood between them. He was saying something. His lips moved, but it was like someone had turned the volume all the way down. She couldn't hear anything.

"Addison, don't do this to me...not again. Wake up. Please," her father pleaded.

She felt herself moving, being pulled off of Luke for a second time. When she opened her eyes again, her father stood between her and Luke. "I think it's best if I check his pulse this time," he said matter-of-factly.

She placed a hand on her father's wrist. "There's no need. He's going to be fine." He turned to her with a puzzled look on his face. She forged a smile, hoping to calm him. "Trust me, Dad. I know." She looked to the side. The bone Luke had found in her vision was not there. She fished her cell phone out of her pocket and dialed. When the operator answered, she simply said, "I need the police and an ambulance. Now."

CHAPTER 40

The ambulance arrived fifteen minutes later, stopping in front of Addison's distraught-looking father, who had been waiting outside the manor. He led them to the place Luke had been found in the woods. Luke was still unconscious when they heaved him onto the stretcher and carried him back to the truck. The EMTs asked questions about what had happened. Addison reassured them that all would be revealed once the police arrived on the scene. She watched the medics take him away, wishing she could go with them and be by his side, but she knew she had to stay until the police arrived. And she didn't have to wait long. Minutes later, a patrol car pulled up. Two officers stepped out and proceeded on foot until they reached Addison in the woods.

"I'm Officer Waters," a woman said. "What's going on here?"

Addison explained how she'd found Luke, not

realizing the barrage of questions she'd just opened herself up to.

"Were you here when it happened?" Officer Waters asked.

Addison shook her head.

"So how did you know he was out here?"

"I…umm…well…he told me."

"When?"

"This morning."

"You saw him earlier today? What time was that?"

"Around nine, I guess."

Officer Waters gave her an icy stare that was more suited for convicted felons than for her. "What did the two of you talk about?"

"He's remodeling my house, so we went over some plans and then I left to meet with someone in the city."

"Who?"

"Why does it matter?"

The second officer spoke up, a male, Officer Jackson, who was even less enthused than his partner. "Why was he even out here, alone, with a shovel?"

Both officers perfected their icy stare, eyeballing Addison for an answer. At the risk of being accused of a crime, she decided she'd had enough questions for one day. She clenched her hands together and said a silent prayer, hoping her gut feeling would pay off. "I need to show you something," she said to both officers.

Officer Jackson looked as if he had a fresh coffee brewing in the car that he needed to get back to. Officer Waters, however, actually looked intrigued. "Let's get on with it."

Addison crouched down, leaning into the hole and digging her fingernails into the dirt while the two officers and her father looked on. Out of the corner of her eye she watched her father swallow—hard. He looked as if his legs were about to buckle beneath him at any moment. She dug out a foot of soil and found nothing. She dug to the left. Nothing.

"What are we supposed to be seeing here?" Officer Jackson grunted.

Addison didn't know how much longer she could keep them there. Then she remembered the words her grandmother said earlier about the power that came with using both of her hands simultaneously. She deliberated the pros and cons in silence, not knowing what would happen if she tried pressing both hands to the ground at the same time. One glance at Officer Waters's look of boredom and she no longer cared. If something was going to happen, it needed to happen now. With one hand firmly stuck inside a cast, she relied on her fingers, hoping it was enough. She flattened her fingers inside the hole and pressed down. After a moment the area to her right gave off a pale glow. Addison glanced up at both officers who looked at each other like they had a crazy woman on their hands. Whatever she was seeing, it was apparent that they didn't. She slid her hand farther right. Something moved.

"I don't know what's going on here, but we need to move on," Officer Jackson said. He turned to her father. "I'll need a number for you two in case we need to get in touch again."

Addison ignored him. She dug two fingers into the ground and wiggled them around until she felt something hard and boney. She pulled up, trusting she wouldn't slip into another one of her visions, and breathed a small sigh of relief when she didn't. Her fisted hand emerged from the ground just in time for Officer Jackson to start walking away.

"You'll want to see this," she shouted.

She unrolled her fingers, lifting her palm into the air for all to see.

Officer Waters glanced at her male counterpart and said, "What the hell?!" She removed some kind of transmitter from her waist belt, pressed a button, and spoke directly into it. "This is Waters. Get McReedy out here right away."

CHAPTER 41

After being grilled for over a half an hour about why Luke was among the trees in the first place, Addison stuck to the same story. She told them Luke had been running earlier that day and thought he saw something sticking out of the ground. He'd returned with a shovel to investigate. As to how he got smacked over the head with it, Addison pled the Fifth. In truth, she herself was interested in the answer to that one.

Before long an entire crew of people arrived, and Addison was pushed back several yards from the place they were now referring to as a possible crime scene. As far as they were concerned, she'd fulfilled her obligations and was no longer needed. They'd take it from here.

"I wonder what will happen now," her father said on their way back to the house.

"I have no idea, but I need to get to Luke, see if he's

all right."

Luke would have to wait a little longer. Waiting inside her house like she owned the place was Addison's neighbor, Helen, who prodded Addison about what was going on in "her" woods. The police had warned Addison not to say anything to anyone until something could be confirmed, and she intended to keep quiet. She still had some investigating of her own to do. Addison simply told Helen that she wasn't sure what was going on. All she knew was what the police had told her—they'd received a tip and had come to check it out. She assured Helen there was nothing to worry about.

"Nothing to *worry* about?" Helen barked. "How can you say that? There's a whole army of them out there messing up those woods."

"I'm sure they're not trying to mess up anything."

"I don't understand," Helen said. "What could possibly be back there?"

Addison glared at her, giving her a look that said, "You know *exactly* what's back there."

Helen appeared to be physically pained that she couldn't walk to the hole and make further inquiries, but her cane kept her on a short leash. Addison possessed neither the time nor the patience to speak with her any longer.

"Wait, where are you going?"

"I have somewhere else I need to be."

"Who's going to watch *them?*" Helen said, her eyes shifting from Addison to the woods.

Addison laughed. "I'm not a babysitter." On that note, she turned to leave and spotted a woman exiting a blue Honda Accord. She didn't think much of it until the woman stepped closer. She had a familiar looking face, and when she flashed a strained smile in Addison's direction, she realized she'd seen her before, in the vision she had when she'd touched Luke in the woods. The woman was the one grinning at her at the beach. She was part of the future. Her future. She had to be. And even though they'd never met, somehow she knew today would be the day they did.

CHAPTER 42

It hadn't been a typical evening for medical examiner, Lia McReedy. When she received a call about possible bones being discovered in the woods of Rhinebeck, she'd chalked it up to nothing more than a couple of police officers who couldn't tell the difference between an animal bone and a human bone. After several years on the job, a dead body had never been dug up before, not in her county, and she had no reason to believe that would all change today.

McReedy arrived at the scene of the so-called crime with every intention of getting in and out within the first fifteen minutes. She had cats to feed, red and black plaid flannel pajamas to don, and a *Criminal Minds* marathon, which had been recording all day. Even now, she could practically taste the saltiness of the pork chops she'd thrown into the crockpot before dashing off to work. Time was of the essence.

As she hiked through the masses of thick, towering trees, she became aware of something: a shadowy presence following close behind. The shadow remained about fifteen feet back and went to great lengths to remain unheard, until the shadow stumbled, nose diving to the ground. She turned, looking the stone-faced girl in the eye. "Are you all right?"

The girl nodded.

"Good. Why are you following me?"

Apprehension cloaked the girl's face like a deer searching for a way out of a blazing forest fire. She stopped. "I…was…ahh…"

McReedy rested both hands on her hips. "You were what?"

"Curious about who you are."

"Why?"

The girl turned and pointed. "I own the house over there. I'm the one who found the ahh…bone."

McReedy glanced at her watch and sighed. "What's your name?"

"Addison Lockhart."

"Well, Addison Lockhart, I need you to return to your house and let me do my job. You can't be back here until we clear out. Got it?"

McReedy waited for Addison to nod and turn before proceeding forward. She wasn't the type of person to have a guilty conscience, but somewhere inside of her she felt the slightest bit guilty about the way she'd treated the girl, who looked to be around her own age. The feeling subsided when she approached the hole.

"What have we got?" she asked.

Officer Waters swiveled around, using her pointer finger as a guide. "See for yourself."

McReedy tipped her head forward expecting to find nothing more than a miniscule pile of weathered bones. The grisly, skeletal remains fused into the dirt proved her wrong. *Criminal Minds* would have to wait.

"What do you make of it?" Officer Waters asked.

"How were these found?"

"We received a call from a woman named Addison Lockhart. She lives in the area. Apparently, the guy who's been doing some work on her home discovered something back here earlier today, and when he brought a shovel out to investigate, someone hit him over the head with it. The girl found him here in this pit and dialed 9-1-1."

"Where is he now?"

"At the hospital, I suppose. We've got a couple officers there waiting to talk to him when he wakes up."

"And the girl?"

Officer Waters shook her head. "Strangest thing. She claims she didn't know a body was back here, but right in front of Jackson and me, she stuck her hand through the dirt and pulled out a bone. Just like that. It was like she knew it would be there."

"And you're not holding her?"

"We've got eyes on her. Nothing's been proven yet. She wants to go to the hospital and visit her handyman. We'll let her. Escorted, of course."

"I wouldn't let her out of your sight. She's a curious one. She knows something. I can tell."

"You do your job and let us do ours," Officer Jackson called from behind.

"Jackass," McReedy mumbled to herself.

"What was that?" Officer Jackson asked.

It had been over seven months since their break-up and Jackson continued to berate her like he still held a place of authority in her life. Never before had any man been so domineering, making her feel like a puppet dangling from a string. Whenever they found themselves together he followed her every movement, his eyes sharp like a hawk, never missing even the minutest details. Back when they lived together she'd plotted her escape, knowing every moment needed to be planned just right. It took months of preparation, and in the end, she didn't just cut away the string, she ripped through it, vowing she'd never allow herself to be under any man's thumb again. She overpowered the hawk by becoming an eagle, an eagle that was flying free.

"At least our cause of death is an easy one," McReedy said, looking at Waters who tried her best to conceal a smile.

"With a big, round hole in the head, I should say not," Waters replied. "The question is, given we don't know how much time these bones have been in the ground, how do you tell whether it's a male or female?"

"Easy," McReedy said. "From the pelvis. There are obvious differences."

"Such as?"

"A male's is narrower, more heart-shaped. A female's is open and circular."

Officer Waters scanned the bones more closely. "So, what I'm looking at is—"

"A probable homicide. The question is—why? And how long have these bones been here?"

CHAPTER 43

Luke was conscious but not full of conversation when Addison arrived. Two officers stood on the sides of his bed, each asking their questions in turns like Bad Cop and Worse Cop.

"We'll ask you one more time, what were you doing out there?" Bad Cop asked.

He didn't answer.

"How'd you know the exact location of those bones?" Worse Cop chimed in.

He didn't answer.

"Who hit you over the head with a shovel?"

No answer.

"You'd better start talking, kid."

The strong scent of Listerine mixed with a heavy application of Giorgio Armani cologne wafted through an otherwise sterile-smelling hall. Addison turned and locked eyes on a slightly overweight fifty-something man coming toward her. He was dressed in a black pinstripe suit and carried a metal container in his hand. Probably coffee. He was not smiling. He passed Addison and winked. It was the kind of wink that commanded a room. She didn't know how, but she was certain everything was about to be all right.

The man entered Luke's room, full vocal chords blazing. Bad Cop and Worse Cop did their best to reason with him, but their efforts were short-lived and to no avail. After a minute, both officers left the room looking like a couple of teenagers who'd been busted for ditching school. Addison wasn't sure what had just happened, but she liked it. She poked her head through the door slowly.

Luke waved her inside. "Get in here. My Uncle Rob wants to meet you."

His uncle?

Uncle Rob advanced toward her. "Robert Flynn. And you are?"

"Addison. Luke is doing some work on my house."

Uncle Rob roared with laughter and looked at Luke. "Do all of your…uh…clients pay you personal visits? Maybe I'm in the wrong business."

Addison's face warmed considerably and she was sure her eyes bulged out just a little. She backed up, wishing she could melt into the floor.

Luke smiled. "I appreciate you coming down here—"

"But you'd like some time with her, eh? One on one?

I get it. My work is done here." He turned to Addison and flipped a business card into her hand. "Lovely to meet you. Should you ever need legal counsel, you know who to call."

Addison leaned out of the doorway and down the hall, making sure he was gone before speaking. "He's…ahh…interesting."

"Yeah, sorry about that."

"What happened?"

"You mean, how'd I get a big knot on my head? I don't know. I didn't hear anyone walk up behind me. Whoever it was knew what was there."

"What time was it—do you remember?"

"Around two or so I guess. Why?"

"That was right before I got home, which explains why your attacker ran off. He must have heard me coming."

"If it's someone who knows what happened all those years ago, he or she isn't exactly a spring chicken—not anymore." He glanced out the window. "What did the cops find—anything?"

"It wasn't what *they* found—it was what *I* found. When I met with my grandmother earlier, she said when I use both of my hands together, I'm more umm, powerful, I guess. I can light stuff up, see things others can't. I pulled a bone right out of the ground."

"Makes sense. When stuff was flying around the

house the day you found out the dress was stolen, you put both of your hands out and that's what stopped everything."

"They're attacking the hole like a colony of ants now. I have no idea what's going on."

"And who's that?" Luke said tilting his head toward the door at a police officer sitting in a padded chair with his head propped against the wall.

"My babysitter. He brought me here and won't let me out of his sight. They must have discovered a lot more once they dug a little deeper. I imagine we're both suspects."

"At least we know what happened to Roxanne Rafferty. We may not know who's responsible, but maybe she'll leave you alone."

"My grandmother knows," Addison blurted.

Luke sat up in bed. "What did she say?"

"Nothing. She just kept asking me to leave Grayson Manor. I asked her why my mother hated that place, and she wouldn't give me an answer. Then when we went to leave the coffee shop, she disappeared as soon as we walked out of the front door."

"So…what now?"

"Now I find her."

CHAPTER 44

When Addison returned home, there were more ants surrounding the hole than ever before. It was dark out, but special lighting had been brought in with the aid of a pair of generators. Her front porch had been transformed into a kind of central police hub, where everyone camped out as they waited. One guy was overheard saying they had almost everything they needed and the bones were ready for transport back to the lab. She hoped that meant they'd be leaving soon. She was tired. Her father had already called it a night, and she could think of nothing better than to follow suit.

Even with all of the chaos, it had been good spending time with her father. His honesty had come at the right time and had left her with a profound desire to explore more about her lineage. She had so many questions and hoped that Marjorie would be able to provide the missing details about the late Miss Rafferty;

perhaps during the process she would learn more about herself and what it meant to be a medium. She also wondered if Marjorie had any information about her grandfather's whereabouts.

Addison brushed past the small crowd and entered the house, shutting and locking the door behind her. Several times over the next hour or so she lifted the drapes and peeked out, delighted to find fewer and fewer cars dotting the landscape. As she stared out the window the fourth time, she saw the woman she had followed earlier that day—the one from her vision on the beach. The woman was arguing with Officer Jackson, but not about the case. It was personal, more intimate—at least on his end. His words were coarse and heavy, hers sharp and to the point.

"Who is he then?" Officer Jackson demanded.

"No one," the woman replied. "I'm not here to discuss my personal life. Excuse me."

She tried to slip by him, but he braced his hands on her shoulders, locking her in place.

She gritted her teeth. "Let go. Now! I'm warning you, TJ."

He didn't. He smiled down at her, his face resembling a slithering snake. The woman glared back. She looked furious—like if she had a gun, she'd blow his head clean off.

Addison opened the door. "Excuse me."

Officer Jackson and the woman both turned, his hands remaining on her shoulders as if they belonged there.

Addison directed her comments to the woman. "Can I ask you a question?" The woman nodded, practically leaping up the porch steps. Officer Jackson followed. The woman slipped inside. The officer tried to do the same, but Addison was quick to shut him down. "Not you. Just her." She slammed the door, sliding the deadbolt into place.

This seemed to impress the woman until she looked at Addison and started talking. "What's your question? I'm in a hurry."

"I don't have one. I just…saw you out there and I…thought you could use a little help. I hope that's okay."

"Are you kidding? It's great." She stuck her hand out. "Sorry I snapped at you. It's been a long day. And he's…well…just made it longer. I'm Lia McReedy."

Addison took Lia's hand in hers. "What's your job, if you don't mind me asking?"

"I examine the bodies."

"Is he…always like that with you?"

Lia tipped her head toward the porch. "TJ?"

Addison nodded.

"We used to be together. He doesn't really grasp the concept of 'broken up.'"

"I've been with a few men like that myself. Can I get

you anything?"

"Coffee, if you have it." Lia followed Addison into the kitchen. "Cool place you've got here."

"I inherited it."

Addison poured two cups of coffee and handed one to Lia. They sat down at the table.

"Can I ask you something?" Lia said.

"Sure."

"How'd you know there was a body back there?"

"I've already given my statement to the officers who were here earlier."

"Yeah, but there's more to it."

Addison raised a brow. "Why do you say that?"

"I can just tell these things. Call it a gift."

A gift. She had no idea.

"Several decades ago, a woman went missing after a party she attended in this house. She was an actress. Roxanne Rafferty."

"Was she ever found?"

Addison shook her head. She told Lia about the dress she'd found after moving in and about the man who posed as a detective. "I don't want to give you the impression that I'm crazy, but the floor in the room upstairs looks like someone cleaned it with bleach."

Both girls walked upstairs slowly, mindful of the fact that Addison's father was sleeping nearby. Addison closed the door and turned on the light. Lia examined the large circle on the faded wood floor.

"Well, what do you think?" Addison asked.

"It's hard to say. I don't think you're crazy, but there's one thing here that doesn't make sense. You said a woman went missing—this Roxanne Rafferty person. But the skeleton behind your house isn't a woman's. It's a man's."

CHAPTER 45

Addison's mind refused to settle, her eyes continually drawn to the time displayed on the clock on her nightstand. It ticked by. Slowly. Effortlessly. She'd struggled for hours to find a comfortable position. She'd even taken something to help her sleep. Nothing worked. Nothing quieted her mind. And she'd come to the conclusion that nothing would. Not tonight.

The bones weren't a woman's. They were a man's. Her grandfather's. She didn't need confirmation. She knew they were his. All of the stories she'd been told since arriving at Grayson Manor swirled around in her head like a blizzard on a cold winter's day, and she couldn't help but come to the decision that every last one had been laced with lies.

She went downstairs, opened the front door and stepped outside, taking in a lungful of precious country air. She wrapped a blanket around her and sat down, allowing her feet to dangle over the front porch steps. Sharing a house with Roxanne had made her weary. She wanted to help her, give her the resolve she needed to move on, but it was hard to know where to go or who to turn to anymore.

She leaned her body against the porch railing and rested her eyes. But not for long. Two hands, heavy and thick thrust down, crushing her ribcage, the force so powerful it flattened her body to the ground. She fought for breath, swallowing big, empty gulps of air. She looked up and saw no one, yet she was stuck, as if the blanket wrapped over her had been nailed into place. Roxanne? No, it couldn't be. She'd always been surrounded by a ray of light and not cloaked in blackness. A figure outlined in black took shape before her. His stone-like eyes were cold and menacing, his lips tight. He removed his hands from her chest and encircled them around her neck, his thumbs pressing into the well in the center, cutting off the airflow throughout her body. *I'm going to die here!* As much as she missed the presence of her mother, she wasn't ready to go—not yet, not like this.

Suddenly, hands were on the back of her shirt, dragging her inside the house—through the front door—to safety. As her body retracted into the entry way, the blackness surged toward the door, then smacked into it and started to fade. Within seconds, it was gone. The door closed, Addison turned. No one was there. She was all alone, yet someone had rescued her. She checked on her father. He was asleep. She wrapped her arms around herself and walked back to her room. Grateful she'd been rescued, she whispered, "Roxanne, I don't know if you can hear me, but if you can, thank you."

CHAPTER 46

Helen, Hugh Brandon, Celeste Brandon, and Marjorie Grayson sat around a circular table. Helen had her hands folded in her lap. Hugh and Celeste rested theirs on the edge of the table. Marjorie's were crossed in front of her. They all stared at one another, but no one said a word. It was like a game really—who goes first?—even though everyone knew Marjorie was the ringleader of the bunch.

Years earlier they had agreed that what really happened the night of Roxanne Rafferty's disappearance would never pass their lips again. They had also agreed that no matter how much time went by, it would be wise for them to keep their distance from one another. Well, all except Hugh and Celeste. After all, they *were* married.

Not to disappoint, Marjorie spoke first. "Honestly Celeste, I really don't know what you were thinking."

Celeste crossed one leg over the other and avoided

Marjorie's gaze. "What do you mean?"

"Dottie Davis? What kind of name is that?"

"A damn good one if you ask me. How was I to know the girl would come here?"

"Dottie Davis doesn't exist!" Marjorie howled. "How long do you think it will take my granddaughter to figure that out?"

"Long enough for us to make a decision. That's what we're here for, aren't we?"

"Which one of you followed me to the coffee shop?"

Hugh raised his pointer finger into the air but didn't say a word.

"And *you*," Marjorie said, shifting her focus to him. "Posing as a detective, stealing the dress, and then hitting that young man over the head with a shovel. What the hell has gotten into you people?!"

Hugh rubbed his hands together as though he was washing them. "He was about to discover Norman's body. I wasn't trying to hurt him. I panicked."

"You were supposed to keep your distance. That's what we agreed upon, remember?"

Helen, who up until now had been quietly taking it all in, slammed a hand down on the table. "All of this might have been avoided if you had burned that dress along with all of the other evidence."

"The dress was my mother's. It's one of the only things I had left of hers. I know it was wrong to keep it.

But after so many years, I never thought it would matter."

"None of us would even be here if it wasn't for you, Marjorie," Helen pointed out.

Marjorie clenched her teeth together, fighting to maintain her composure. "Meaning?"

"The reason the girl came here in the first place is because she inherited that house. *Your* house. If anyone is to blame in all of this, it's you. It was bad enough when Detective Dobbs wouldn't stop sniffing around all those years ago. Now your own granddaughter is playing detective!"

Marjorie leaned back in the chair and rubbed circles around her eyes with her fingers. "My daughter died—I always assumed she wouldn't ever care to go back there. I figured by the time I passed on, it wouldn't matter anymore. I was wrong."

Hugh laughed. "You were *wrong*? I never thought I'd see the day."

All three women glared at him. None of them smiled.

"If you're quite done, Hugh, we have a decision to make," Marjorie said.

"I still think we could drive her away from that house," he said.

"We can't. Nothing will make her leave. Not now."

Hugh sighed. "How can you be so sure?"

It was a question she couldn't answer. Not with the

truth. Explaining Addison's ability was something she'd never do—they wouldn't understand anyway. No one ever did. The spirit of Roxanne Rafferty was alive and well at Grayson Manor, and there was only one way to get her out. "I met with my granddaughter yesterday, as you all know. I didn't just ask her to leave, I begged her. She refused. Norman's body was dug up by investigators last night. Even if my granddaughter left now, it would be too late. There will be more questions, and Addison won't know how to answer them. The manor will be searched again." Marjorie paused and glanced at each one of them. "And you all know we can't allow that to happen. A lot has changed since Roxanne died. Forensics is far more advanced than it used to be, and this time, we won't be able to stop them from finding the evidence."

Celeste nodded. "We need to tell Addison the truth. It's time."

"And then what—she goes to the police?" Helen threw her hands in the air.

Celeste shrugged her shoulders. "What can they do to us now? It's a risk, but we don't have much choice."

Marjorie stood. "Well then, are we all in agreement?"

Celeste looked at Hugh, who looked at Helen. Helen clasped her hands together and hissed a low but audible, "Fine. We'll tell her. But the moment it goes south, so do I."

CHAPTER 47

When Addison woke the next morning, she found a note taped to the inside of her bedroom door. She had no idea how anyone had gotten in. The night before, she'd locked herself inside, checking the lock three times before crawling back into bed. The note was handwritten in straight, cursive lines. *A woman?* It said: Coffee Shop. 10 AM. COME ALONE. The note was signed "M." *Hmm. M for Marjorie?*

Addison got dressed, told her father she was going to town to get some groceries, and made it all the way to her car before Luke stopped her. "Where you off to?"

"Grocery store."

"You've got plenty of food in that kitchen of yours, and I haven't seen you cook much since you got here."

She shrugged. "I'm in the mood for something different."

"Fine. Mind if I tag along? I forgot to grab something

I needed at the hardware store."

"I'm not sure I'm going that—"

Luke swung the passenger door open and got in. "Let's go."

They drove for almost fifteen minutes before Addison couldn't take it any longer. "How did you know?"

"I'm not sure what I *know* exactly, only that grocery shopping has never been high on your priority list. Especially at this hour. So, where are we going?"

She handed over the note.

"And you really thought going alone was a good idea?"

She took a deep breath. "I'm all out of ideas. That body in the woods, it's a man, not a woman. My guess? My grandfather."

"If he's out there, where's Roxanne?"

"I'm hoping that's what we're about to find out."

***

Marjorie stood in front of the coffee house/soup kitchen modeling a pair of black sunglasses that were so large she looked like she was in the Witness Protection Program. When she got an eyeful of Luke crossing the street with Addison, her words shot out like rapid fire. Addison held a hand up and firmly stated, "He stays or I go. I don't want to do whatever this is without him."

"He shouldn't be here," Marjorie stated. "I know nothing about him."

"And I know almost nothing about you. So what's it going to be?"

Marjorie huffed a few times then said, "Follow me then."

The three of them walked to the park across the street. Once there, Marjorie took them down a secluded path that seemed to lead to nowhere, but when they rounded the corner, Addison couldn't believe the three people sitting on a bench in front of her. She never thought she'd see them in the same room, let alone out together.

"I don't understand," Addison said.

"We'll explain everything," Marjorie said. "I need you to be patient."

"Who's he and why is he here?" Helen said, bending a finger toward Luke.

"No one. Don't worry about him," Marjorie replied.

"Who are *you?*" Addison said to the man sitting between Helen and Celeste Brandon.

"Hugh."

"Hugh Brandon?"

He smiled like she'd just recognized he once was a famous celebrity. "I can't imagine what these three have filled your head with lately. You'll forgive them for a few white lies, won't you?"

"Is this supposed to be funny?" Addison said.

"Look, no one is around right now, and I'm catching a chill," Helen said. "We need to get on with it."

Addison and Luke sat with Marjorie on a bench directly across from the other one.

"She's my granddaughter," Marjorie said. "It might be best if I tell it."

Helen rolled her eyes but said nothing.

"On the night of the party that Roxy went missing, all of us were there."

Addison crossed her arms in front of her. "So basically you *have* all been lying to me about everything."

"Interrupting me won't change things now," Marjorie replied. "Do you want to hear the story or don't you?" She gave her words time to sink in and then continued. "Your grandfather was having an affair with Roxy and had been for some time. I knew, of course, as did most everyone. He had quite the reputation with the ladies back then. He made them all kinds of promises to further their careers, and they fell for it. Every last one. Imagine their dismay when, after one or two bit parts in small films, he moved on with someone else."

"Roxanne didn't have small roles," Addison said.

"Roxy was different. You see, your grandfather liked to be in charge. And when he wasn't, well, let's just say it drove him to do things none of us imagined."

"Do you mean to say he shot her out of jealousy?" Addison asked.

Marjorie shook her head. "Not exactly."

"What then?"

"The night of the party, Roxy showed up, even though she hadn't been invited. I had a firm rule about him bringing any of his flings to the house. They weren't allowed. But that didn't stop her. She came anyway. She asked if she could talk to me. So, we went into another room away from everyone else, and she confessed to the affair. She wasn't aware, of course, that I already knew she'd been seeing him."

"Was it you, then? Did you shoot her?"

Marjorie tossed her head back and laughed. "Heavens, no. She asked for my forgiveness, and although I didn't give it to her, I respected her for having the decency to tell me the truth—and to my face, no less. She said she only came over to break off the affair and to clear things up with me and with him."

"And did she?"

"I counseled her not to tell him that night. He'd been drinking, and I knew how he could be when he didn't get his way. She thought she could reason with him—she said she had to. She'd met someone else. Someone she didn't have to sneak around with."

"Did she tell him?"

"As soon as he saw her he went on the attack, airing

it all out in front of our guests. I took him aside and gave him two options: leave the house or take her to another room, somewhere more discreet. A few minutes later, he rejoined our guests. Roxy was nowhere to be seen, but no one saw her leave. The party wound down after another hour or so, and I saw Norman heading upstairs. He'd had a lot to drink and could barely walk. I assumed he was going to bed."

"I know about the blood on the floor in my mother's room."

Marjorie patted Addison's leg. "You're getting ahead of yourself." She cleared her throat and continued. "A few minutes after he'd gone upstairs I heard two people arguing. And I recognized Roxy's voice. We all assumed she'd gone upstairs to wait it out, thinking perhaps if he sobered up, she could talk to him."

"Where was my mother?"

"I used to put her in the bedroom at the end of the hall when we had parties because it was the quietest room in the house. I should have thought to check on her, but I didn't. My only concern at the time was getting everyone out so I could deal with another one of his messes."

Addison looked at the others. "So everyone left except the three of you?" They all nodded in agreement.

"I was saying goodbye to a friend when I heard a gunshot go off," Marjorie said. "Several seconds went by and I heard another. The four of us practically stepped over each other to get up those stairs. I flung your mother's door open and stood there. Shocked. We all were. Norman and Roxy were both dead."

"I don't understand," Addison said. "Did one shoot the other and then turn the gun on themselves?"

"No, dear."

"What then?"

"Roxy shot your grandfather."

"Then…who shot Roxy?"

There was an unsettling silence before Hugh spoke up for all of them. "Your mother."

CHAPTER 48

"*My mother?* She was just a child. How is that even—"

"Possible?" Hugh answered. "The four of us talked it over many times after it happened. We think Norman pulled a gun on Roxy, and she charged at him. The gun went off, killing him. Their arguing probably woke your mother. She came into the room at some point—we don't know whether it was before or after. When Roxy realized what she'd done, we think she dropped the gun. Your mother picked it up, and when she saw her father dead on the ground, she aimed the gun at Roxy."

"Unfortunately, she had very good aim," Helen added. "The single shot killed Roxy immediately."

"And my mother?" Addison asked. "Where was she?"

"All curled up in the corner of the room, crying."

"So you see," Helen said, "it was an accident. Your mother probably didn't mean to shoot her. She got scared. Your father was her whole world. She was only trying to protect him. She didn't know Roxy had only been trying to defend herself."

"But why not tell the police? What would they possibly do to a child?"

"That's just it," Marjorie said. "We didn't know what they'd do. And we weren't about to risk it. Our primary concern was to protect your mother. We couldn't imagine all the questions the police would have asked her, or how many times they would have grilled her, making her relive the events over and over again. I couldn't put her through that."

"So what did you do?" Addison asked.

Marjorie spoke up. "I had her stay with Helen while I dealt with the police. When all the fuss died down and we'd destroyed the evidence, I left Grayson Manor knowing I would never return. The four of us made a deal to never mention what happened again."

"Did my mother ever tell you what actually happened?"

"She didn't," Marjorie said. "In fact, I did everything I could to help her forget it, but I know she never did."

Luke leaned forward. "We know Addison's grandfather was buried in the woods. What we don't know is—what did you do with Roxanne Rafferty?"

CHAPTER 49

Luke, Addison, and Marjorie stood next to the wine racks at the back of the hidden room. Addison's father had received an invitation to join Helen for dinner, an offer he couldn't refuse.

"So where's Roxanne?" Addison asked.

Marjorie bent her head to one side. Addison didn't follow. Marjorie bent her head again, this time a little more.

"You're telling me, she's in *there*?" Addison pointed. "In the wall?! No wonder she can't move on."

Marjorie shrugged. "I had no way of knowing she'd be stuck here, in this life. I mean, it crossed my mind, but you need to understand—time was essential. We had to make a decision. I'm not proud of what I've done."

"Why not bury her in the woods next to my grandfather?"

"Hugh and Celeste dealt with him, and Helen and I

dealt with her. We decided not to tell each other what we'd done in case one of the bodies was discovered. The less people involved the better."

Addison sized up the brick wall. "What exactly did you do?"

"This room used to be two feet wider. So we just…"

Luke felt up and down the bricks. "Stuck her inside and sealed it up. Do you see the way this is cracking? I bet I can pull some of these bricks out with my fingers."

"We need to get her out," Addison insisted.

"We can't. Not now that Norman's body has been found. The police will be back, this time with even more zest than before. We have no choice. Roxy may be uneasy, but she'll just have to wait."

"We can't wait."

"And why not?"

"Because Roxanne's spirit isn't the only one that's uneasy."

Marjorie squinted. "What do you mean?"

Addison told her what she had experienced the night before.

"Norman knows Roxy's spirit is still here," Marjorie said. "She killed him, and now that he has been freed, he's come back for her." She was quiet for a time. "I'll need your help to get rid of him for good, but Roxy's body stays until I see fit to let her go."

"No!"

A startled Marjorie took a step back. Luke smiled.

"This isn't up to you," Addison said. "This is my house now. I'm setting her free."

"You don't know what you're doing, Addison. Roxy doesn't know who killed her. You might think she's not a vengeful spirit, but trust me. She is."

Addison faced Marjorie. "Here's what's going to happen. You are going to write a letter, and you're going to leave it with me. Then I want you to disappear. Go somewhere for a while and don't come back until all of this has blown over." She turned to Luke. "I want you to pick up my father. Take him into town. Do something with him—anything. Just make sure he's clear of the house until you hear from me."

***

Marjorie and Addison sat in the center of the floor in her mother's old room, their hands joined together, eyes closed.

"Are you ready?" Marjorie asked.

"Ready."

"Whatever you do, don't break hold. We will do our part. What happens after that is up to them."

"Have you done this before?"

"No. But when my mother was alive, she did it with her mother, and they taught me how."

Addison flinched. No matter how hard she tried, she

couldn't shake the queasy, curdled-milk feeling inside of her. This was it. She could feel Roxanne nearby, her spirit wandering to and fro, as if pacing the room.

Marjorie began. "Norman Grayson, we invite you in."

Several seconds passed. Nothing happened. Addison half opened one eye and leaned forward. "That's it? That's all you're going to say?"

Marjorie shook her head, silencing Addison. "Norman Grayson, I command you to appear."

The bedroom light went out. Darkness spread across the room, and from it, the spirit of Addison's grandfather rose up through the planks of wood, his body twisting and turning to break free. His head swiveled around, taking in his surroundings. A devilish grin ripped across his face. He'd been waiting for this moment for a long time, and it was finally here.

He didn't seem to notice Addison and Marjorie at first. When he did, his face shot forward in an instant, hovering only a few inches in front of Addison. His mouth opened, but he didn't speak. He cackled, his head looming in front of her like he wanted to crawl inside of her mind. She had the urge to let go of her grandmother's hands and swish her hands in front of her, fending him off. Then she remembered her grandmother's words: *Whatever you do, don't break hold.*

Just when she thought he couldn't come any closer, his head twisted around, his eyes falling upon Marjorie like a pair of daggers. Marjorie opened her eyes. Met his gaze. And then she gave him a look that reeked of sweet revenge. She glanced down, enticing him to follow her gaze, to see her hands entwined with Addison's, bound as one.

The smug grin left his face.

Light entered the room, just as it had the first night Roxanne had appeared at the end of Addison's bed. No longer did Roxanne look like a spirit; she looked human, like Addison could reach out and touch her, feel her flesh. Norman's hands shot out in front of him, his hands gripping Roxanne's neck. Her light started to fade. Roxanne looked at him, then at Addison. She reached her hand out toward her.

"Take it," Marjorie said.

"But I thought you said—"

"We cannot help those in darkness. Only those on the side of the light. She is full of light. I can see that now. She needs you, Addison."

Addison didn't think—she reacted, locking hands with Roxanne. Roxanne flattened her free hand in front of her, spreading her fingers apart. A white orb formed inside her palm. She made a fist and then thrust her hand into Norman's chest. She uncurled her fingers and released the orb inside him. He writhed, trying to shake her off, but it was too late. Light coursed through his body, growing brighter until it burst, spreading tiny fragments of white crystals throughout the air.

The room returned to normal. Addison's grandfather was gone, but Roxanne remained. Marjorie released Addison's hand and stood. "She came to you. Only you can help her get to where she needs to be."

"I don't even know what I'm doing. Do I have to do it alone?"

"You don't need me anymore—not for this. Trust yourself. Believe in yourself." She walked to the door and turned. "I'm very proud of you, Addison. You've grown into a strong, beautiful woman, just like your mother. Let your strength be your guide."

The door closed. Addison rose, facing Roxanne. "I'm not really sure how to do this, or what to say, but here it goes. Your death was an accident. Since then, you've been trapped here. You didn't get the respect or the recognition you deserved. I'm sorry for what was done to you. And if you let me, I will make sure you are honored and put you in a place where others can honor you too. You're free, Roxanne. Free to leave this life and this house. It's time for you to move on. Don't be afraid."

Addison stepped back as if expecting some kind of magical light to appear. It didn't. But something else did. A door, shiny and white, where the window in the room used to be. It opened. Addison saw nothing but pure white light on the other side.

Roxanne saw something different. She hoisted a hand into the air and began waving. Tears rolled down both sides of her cheeks. She ran to the door, stopping for a brief moment to turn back and look at Addison. "Thank you," she said.

A moment later, both the door and Roxanne were gone.

CHAPTER 50

Lia McReedy sat on Addison's sofa, one leg bent under the other, arms crossed, eyes glued to a piece of paper in front of her dated October 1952. She chewed the inside of her mouth as she read a letter that started: *It is out of the guilt in my heart that I write this letter.* When she finished, she folded the letter, set it on her leg and looked over. "Where did you find this?"

"I was looking through an old chest in a storage room and it was on the inside of my grandmother's wedding album," Addison replied.

"Why show it to me first and not the police?"

"I guess I felt more comfortable calling you. I hope that's okay."

"You understand what this means, right?"

Addison nodded. "Roxanne Rafferty shot my grandfather in self-defense. My mother, who was a child at the time, shot Roxanne, and my grandmother covered it up. She buried Norman in the woods and Roxanne in the basement."

Lia tapped the side of her cheek with a finger. "It's so odd to me that she didn't just bury the bodies together. And your mother never mentioned it to anyone—not even when she was an adult?"

"Not to me or my father."

Addison's father, who had been sitting quietly in an armchair, spoke up. "It's true. This is the first I've heard of it."

"Why do you think your grandmother wrote it down?"

Addison shrugged. "She probably wished she could tell someone, but there wasn't anyone she could trust."

"So…where's your grandmother now?"

Addison exchanged glances with her father. "I don't know. We haven't seen her in years."

***

A few hours later, Grayson Manor was once against bombarded with various representatives of the police department. Luke stated that after he'd read the letter Addison shared with him, he'd done a little digging in the hidden storage room. He said it hadn't taken much to take apart some of the brick wall and that a single glow from his flashlight attested to the truth of Marjorie's letter—there were the remains of a body, wrapped in plastic, behind the wall. What followed was a media frenzy that went viral—one that would forever label Grayson Manor as a "haunted house." Addison didn't care. The opinions of others mattered little to her now.

CHAPTER 51

(Three months later)

Addison, Luke, Hugh and Celeste Brandon, and Helen stood together in front of Roxanne Rafferty's headstone. In unison, they bowed their heads and paid their last respects by offering a moment of silence in her honor. And although Marjorie was not in attendance, Addison felt her presence, certain she was somewhere nearby, watching and perhaps offering some kind of respect of her own.

The buzz surrounding the double murder had finally started to die down—not completely—but enough to allow Addison the space she needed to breathe again. Luke continued to work on the house, and sometimes, she even joined him.

When the moment of silence was over, Addison lifted her head. A conversation started about the quote Addison had requested to be etched beneath Roxanne's name on her headstone: *Life every man holds dear; but the dear man holds honor far more precious dear than life - Shakespeare.* Addison, however, wasn't reading along with the group. She was staring off into the distance, watching two little girls in matching yellow dresses chase each other around a headstone. It seemed so odd that they'd been left unattended. *Where is their mother?* Addison looked around. She saw no one. The girls stopped as if realizing they were being watched. They joined hands and stared directly at her. One waved. Then they took a step back and disappeared. Addison squeezed her eyes shut and opened them again. They were gone.

"Are you all right?" Luke asked.

She entwined her hands in his and they walked back to the car. "I'm...fine, I think. I thought I just saw—"

"What?"

"Nothing. Can I ask you something?"

"Anything," he replied. "You know that."

"Have you ever been to the beach?"

***

All of Cheryl Bradshaw's novels are heavily researched, proofed, edited, and professionally formatted. Should you find any errors, please contact the author directly. Her assistant will forward the issue(s) to the publisher. It's our goal to present you with the best possible reading experience, and we appreciate your help in making that happen. You can contact the author through her website, www.cherylbradshaw.com.

***

For updates on Cheryl and her books:

Blog
cherylbradshawbooks.blogspot.com

Web
cherylbradshaw.com

Facebook
facebook.com/#!/CherylBradshawBooks

Twitter
twitter.com/#!/cherylbradshaw

***

Printed in Great Britain
by Amazon